the prayer

Laurie Ann Staples

ISBN: 1545064466
ISBN 13: 9781545064467
Library of Congress Control Number: 2017905118
CreateSpace Independent Publishing Platform
North Charleston, South Carolina

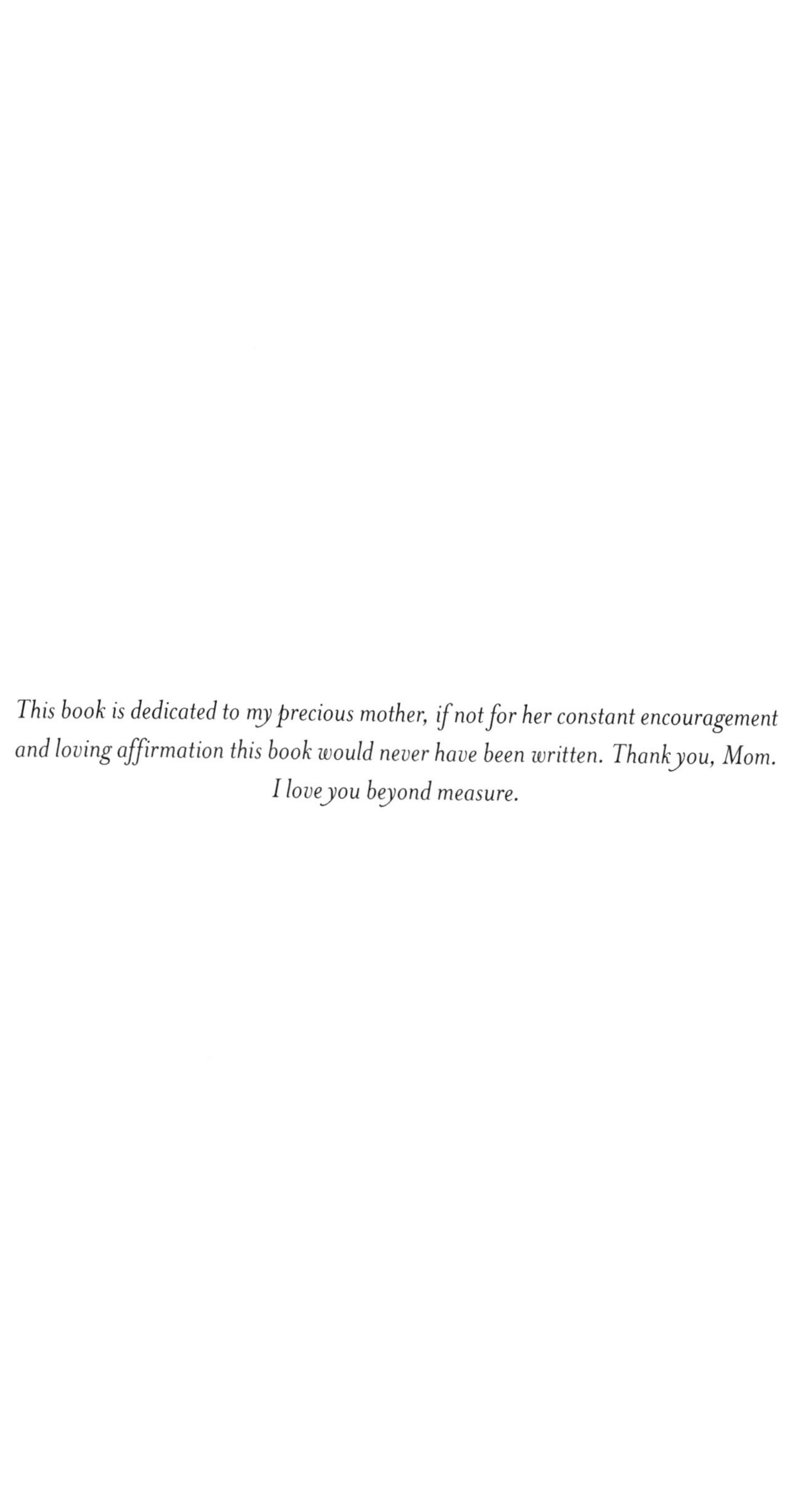

This book is dedicated to my precious mother, if not for her constant encouragement and loving affirmation this book would never have been written. Thank you, Mom. I love you beyond measure.

He does not treat us as our sins deserve
or repay us according to our iniquities,
For as high as the heavens are above the earth,
so great is His love for those who fear Him;
As far as the east is from the west,
so far has He removed our transgressions from us.
—Psalm 103:10–12

Prologue

Love me tender,
Love me sweet,
Never let me go.
You have made my life complete,
And I love you so.

Love me tender,
Love me true,
All my dreams fulfill,
For my Darlin' I love you,
And I always will.

Love me tender,
Love me long,
Take me to your heart,
For it's there that I belong
And will never part.

Love me tender,
Love me dear,
Tell me you are mine
I'll be yours through all the years,
Till the end of time.

—-Elvis Presley

December 15th, 1959

She had conjured up a thousand different images of what this day would be like. Nothing was as she'd imagined. She was alone, for one thing. Not even dear Eva was with her. Eva said a "team of wild horses" couldn't keep her away, yet a distant aunt was dying and off she went to be with the family. She chose to be a part of ushering someone out of this world rather than being here to usher one in. Of course, Eva couldn't have known Janet would go early. It figures a long lost relation would materialize out of thin air just when Janet needed Eva the most.

Her parents had promised to be here, too. But of course they hadn't planned on her going early either. Supposedly, that never happened with a first baby. They'd planned on being here a full week before the baby was due and stay with her until she was well enough to make the trip home. So, unless her labor lasted another nine hours or so *—please God, don't let that happen—* they wouldn't be here either. Nope, she was all alone, but she was determined to be strong.

There wasn't a solitary object of warmth or beauty in the small room they'd put her in. The walls were painted what must have once been white. There was a yellowed shade pulled down past the sill, allowing only the tiniest sliver of dawn light to shine through.

Her eyes were drawn involuntarily to the clock on the wall. It was the same industrial style clock that hung in the classrooms at school. She remembered watching those clocks in school, wishing that by some kinetic power she could make the hands sweep around the face in record time so she could be back with Brett. Oh, what she wouldn't give to turn back the hands of time and be sitting in one of her classes right now—with nothing more important weighing on her mind than what she was going to wear to school the next day.

Instead she was here, in a dreary hospital room, dreading every tick, knowing each second brought her closer to another painful contraction. The pain was so much worse than she'd imagined it would be.

She wouldn't have thought it possible for her belly to get as tight and hard as a watermelon, and cause such indescribable pain in the process. Every five minutes, as predictable as the sun rising in the east. How interesting God had created such an orderly universe. Everything in its time. Just as old Solomon wisely noted, "a time to be born and a time to die, a time to plant and a time to uproot, a time to kill and a time to heal, a time to weep and a time to laugh, a time to mourn and a time to dance . . ." Had she bypassed her time of laughing and dancing?

She tried not watching the clock, but that proved impossible. Whether you wanted to stop time or hurry it along, it always marched on in the same cadence. Never changing. It only *seemed* to go faster when you wanted it to stop entirely.

Janet remembered watching movies depicting births. She had scoffed at the dramatic display of supposedly excruciating pain. All the moaning, screaming and crying seemed a little beyond the pale. She'd smugly believed she was above such drama and when she first started having contractions, she was rather disdainful. ***This*** *was it? This was the reason for all that carrying on?*

She wasn't feeling smug now. She tensed as the second hand inched towards the dreaded minute. With eyes tightly shut and fingers gripping the sheet until her knuckles were white, she braced herself for the next contraction.

The doctor paused unobserved in the doorway. He took in the sight of the young girl in such obvious pain. She was lovely. Her hair must have been pinned up at one point, but now most of it fell around her shoulders in corkscrew tendrils. It was honey gold, with streaks of white blond. She was biting her bottom lip and her eyes were tightly closed. There were little beads of perspiration above her lips. When the pain finally subsided, she sighed and slowly opened her eyes, widening them when she saw him.

Obviously, she hadn't heard him walk in. He was struck by how beautiful her eyes were. Who could have left this stunning young beauty to endure this on her own? He pulled himself together, remembering he was here to help her, not stand there gawking at her beauty and conjecturing about how she came to be here.

"Hi there," he greeted her warmly. "I'm doctor Jack Richardson. I've brought something to help you with the pain. I promise you'll feel better in a matter of minutes." He spoke softly, sympathetically. His kind voice brought tears to her eyes. She didn't trust herself to talk, her chin quivered as she nodded gratefully.

"How far apart are your contractions?"

"Five minutes," she answered weakly, looking at the clock. Three minutes and fifteen more seconds.

He gently fitted a mask over her nose and mouth and asked her to breathe normally. Eager for relief, she gulped in air, inhaling as deeply as she could.

"Tell me when you feel your toes tingling," the doctor instructed.

Janet nodded obediently, then looked back at the clock, resenting every tick. The baby inside of her would soon be making his or her debut, and she would no longer have the miracle of life moving within her.

As she waited for the anesthetic to take effect, she studied the young doctor. He was busy writing something on her chart. The surge of grateful admiration she felt for him made it easy to understand how women fell for their doctors. Especially ones as boyishly handsome as this one. His looks didn't hold a candle to Brett's dark good looks, but still . . . he was definitely appealing.

Thinking of Brett made her consider how thrilling this could have been under different circumstances. She could imagine Brett's awe in placing his hand on her stomach and feeling the little elbow or knee implausibly visible through her skin. She could imagine him being with her now, encouraging her for bravely enduring the pain to bring into the world what their love had created.

Janet forced herself out of her reverie . . . *as it turned out, he hadn't loved her after all. It had* ***seemed*** *so real, so inexplicably perfect. Had it ever been real?*

She couldn't suppress a moan of pain. *Please God, let this be over.* She thought the pain of never seeing Brett again was the worst pain she'd ever have to endure. Now she wasn't so sure.

Two nurses came in and made preparations around her. She was drifting in and out of sleep, no longer able to focus on the clock well enough to see when the next contraction was coming. Not too much longer, they assured her.

"Come on Janet, you're doing great . . . just one more big push and it will all be over." The nurses had been kind and sweet to Janet. She felt a rush of gratitude for these capable strangers. She'd been afraid they'd have a scornful and judgmental attitude, a "serves her right for being such a bad girl" type of thing. But, blessedly, they were treating her like any other young mother delivering her first baby.

Janet stoically tried to comply with all the directives they were giving her. She was so sleepy she was having difficulty focusing on her pushing. Yet her excitement to see her baby was keeping her just alert enough to know what was going on. She was anxious, more anxious than she'd dreamed she could be—she *needed* to know their baby was okay.

"Come on, Janet. Stay with us, you're almost there. Concentrate on pushing . . ."

Janet forced herself to focus, and then, miraculously, she heard the indescribably precious cry of a newborn.

"You did great, Janet! A beautiful, healthy baby girl." The nurse held the baby up so Janet could see her.

Janet was overcome with awed emotion. Surely there was no greater joy than giving birth to a healthy baby! She couldn't choke back the tears, such a miracle! *Thank you, Lord! She's beautiful.* Janet was losing the battle to stay awake. She couldn't get her mouth to work. She wanted to tell them she'd changed her mind, she wouldn't be giving her baby up after all. She wanted to hold her. *Bring her closer, let me see her, let me hold her!* Her arm felt like it weighed fifty pounds, she couldn't get her hand up to remove the mask. She ached to hold her. *Our perfect baby girl, so tiny, so beautiful . . .* She gave in to the drug and drifted into a deep sleep.

The doctor awaited the delivery of the afterbirth, pleased with how smoothly things were going. He was puzzled at the strength of her contractions. These contractions seemed as strong as . . . "Lois!" he called out to the nurse. "I need you back here, there's another baby!"

Lois hurried over, laying the baby in the bassinet, before grabbing a clean receiving blanket for the second baby. This one slipped out more easily. Another baby girl, smaller and not as healthy looking as the first. But, as if to prove them wrong, she let out an angry cry, thoroughly perturbed at being brought out of the warm cocoon of her mother's womb.

There weren't many twins born in their little hospital; they caused quite a stir. The entire staff wanted to see these small miracles, two perfect little baby girls born just minutes apart.

The mother hadn't known there would be twins, and hadn't been conscious when the second one came. The staff was strictly advised not to bring any of the babies to the mothers from The Haven. Seeing and holding their babies made the decision to give them up for adoption much more difficult. It was easier if the birth mother and baby didn't have a chance to bond. Maybe it would be easier for the girl not to know she'd given birth to twins.

When Janet woke up, the sun was going down. How long had she slept? She was so sore. Oh, but it had been worth it! Her heart felt like it could burst with the joy and love she felt at producing a healthy baby girl. Everything was going to be fine. She knew with certainty she could not give her baby up. Once her parents saw her they wouldn't want Janet to give her up either.

Janet couldn't bear the thought of missing her first smile, her first steps, her first words. Her parents would have to agree with her, she was their *granddaughter* for heaven's sake! Hope and possibilities continued to race through her mind as she waited for someone to place her precious bundle in her arms.

A nurse came in with a tray of food. "I bet you're hungry! You had quite a day, but you did wonderfully. You'll be up and about in no time." She spoke cheerily. No mention of the baby.

"Oh, no. I couldn't possibly eat until I've held my baby. I've been waiting so eagerly, could you please bring her to me, I'd . . ."

The nurse cut her off mid-sentence, asking her gently, "you remember how we told you any contact between the birth mother and baby makes the separation more difficult?"

"I know, I remember. But you see, I've changed my mind. I've decided I can't do it. I just can't, please . . ."

"Surely," the nurse interrupted her. "You don't expect to devastate this poor couple now? After all the time and preparations they've made for her? They are elated she has finally arrived."

"I am sorry, but that *is* what I feel I must do. So, please, could you bring her to me?" Janet painfully tried to sit up straighter in the bed. She suddenly felt light hearted, happier than she'd felt in months, thrilled at the miracle of birth and feeling certain God had given her a clear answer to her prayers. She was a mother! A mother with a beautiful baby girl. The two of them could withstand anything together. She would do whatever was necessary to bring her sweet baby up in a thriving, loving environment. No sacrifice would be too big.

The nurse was getting agitated. *What was the problem with her?*

"Miss Roberts . . ." she began sternly.

Janet didn't miss the slight the nurse meant for her to feel with the emphasis on the word "Miss."

"I am sorry that you've had a change of heart," the nurse continued, "but I do have to follow instructions. I think you have visitors eager to see you . . ." she tried to end on a more encouraging note as she finished up her duties and walked out of the room.

"No, bring her to me . . . *please*. . ." Janet whispered as tears fell down her cheeks. When the door closed, great, wrenching sobs engulfed her. *Please God, please let them understand I can't give my baby away.*

The door swung open and her parents, alarmed, rushed to her bedside.

"Janet, please honey, you can't upset yourself like this," her father pleaded.

"I can't do it. I'm sorry, I just can't," Janet cried. "Please make them bring her to me. I have to at least hold her, memorize what she looks like."

Her mother was overwhelmed with compassion for Janet. Watching the despair on her face was heartrending. She looked so pitiful and immature. It was awful she'd had to endure all this pain and anxiety on her own, such a stark contrast to the joy and intimacy Janet's birth had brought her and Don.

It pricked Maggie's conscience that they'd never told her how desperate Brett had been to talk to her. He had written dozens of letters, pleading with them to tell him where she'd gone.

Of course, he never knew anything about the baby. That's what Janet had wanted and they'd obliged. Don hadn't been convinced it was necessary to keep even his letters from Janet, but Maggie had been adamant.

Why? Maggie wondered now. Why had she been so adamant about keeping them apart? Was it because she thought she was saving Janet from a less than perfect love match? Janet had been emphatic about not letting Brett know about the baby. But he'd *seemed* so genuinely heartbroken. It was hard to believe he'd fallen out of love with Janet as she had so hysterically insisted.

Maggie knew, deep down, even if Brett *did* still love her, she wanted something better for Janet. She didn't want her to suffer through a shotgun wedding with the whole town whispering about how shameful it was. She could just hear the criticism—"*I always knew they gave her too much freedom . . . letting her spend time alone with that boy they knew darn well hadn't darkened the door of a church in years. Shameful! They have no one but themselves to blame.*" Oh yes, Maggie could hear all the wagging tongues. It would all come back on her and Don. It would be *their* fault for not properly raising their only child.

Surely it wasn't just her own selfish pride that didn't want to be judged? The thought of her only daughter and granddaughter being treated like second-class citizens the rest of their lives was unthinkable.

She felt if Janet settled for Brett she would miss out on God's best. She was convinced giving the baby up for adoption was the only way Janet could start anew, to truly get a second chance.

But seeing Janet now, so determined to keep her baby, made her second-guess her decision. She felt a stab of guilt and something akin to fear that her choice to keep Brett at bay would come back to haunt her.

Thankfully, Janet never once asked about him. She had resolved to move on with her life without him. She'd always been a strong-willed child. Once she decided something, it'd been awfully difficult to talk her out of it.

"Sweetheart," Don gently pushed a damp curl off her forehead. "You're exhausted and overly emotional after all you've been through. Let's let the doctor bring you something to help you relax a little and then we'll come back and talk about it."

"No. I want to settle it now . . . before they take her somewhere else . . ." Janet looked to her mother for support. "Mama? Please say *you* at least understand. You do don't you? You *must.* You've been through this . . . could *you* have given *me* up?"

Her mother wouldn't even look at her! Tears were rolling down her cheeks as well, but she continued to look down at her hands tightly clasped in front of her. "I can't . . ." she struggled to get the words out. "I can't say what I . . ." She took a deep, steadying breath before lifting her gaze to Janet. "You have to do what you promised. You've given your word. You've signed papers. You have to trust God for the rest."

"But there are plenty of cases where mothers have changed their minds. This is just going to have to be one of them. You have to understand . . . you *must,*" Janet tearfully pleaded, desperate to convince them.

"We're going to let you get some rest, and then we'll be back to talk," her father gently insisted.

Janet continued to stare at her mother, willing her to look back. If she could convince her mother, she knew she would have a staunch ally who would fight with her to the finish. Her mother finally turned to look at her, "Janet, you've got to stop thinking about yourself and more about that baby. You're in no position to give that baby the best. I want you to think about that and we'll talk more tomorrow." She gently kissed her on the cheek and then walked away. She walked away! How could she? Her mother who had stood by her through all of this. How could she walk away *now*, when she needed her most?

The nurse walked in and gave her some medicine and a glass of water. As Janet swallowed the pills, her father stood to leave too.

"We'll see you in the morning, honey," he whispered as he affectionately squeezed her shoulder and walked purposely out of the room.

"Wait . . ." Fresh tears welled in her eyes as she watched her father leave. She despondently looked out the window, tears dampening the pillowcase beneath her. She was suddenly sure she wasn't going to get any support from her parents. *Please God, let them see I can't follow through with this and live another happy day. Let them see I am willing and able to do* ***anything*** *to keep her.*

As Janet continued to stare out the window, she couldn't help thinking about what *could* have been . . .

April 1958

Janet forced herself to go to the basketball game with her friends. She knew she didn't get out enough. She spent way too much time at home with her nose stuck in a book. Her friends teased her about it. How would she ever live a life like the characters in her novels if she stayed home every weekend? So here she was, half watching a purportedly exciting game while trying to write an essay for her English class. She was so involved with her writing she didn't even realize when the game ended.

Her friends were impatient to get out and socialize. That's what they'd come for, right? Janet urged them to go on ahead, she'd finish this last paragraph and catch up with them.

She gathered her things together and started to walk out of the gym, when some guy called out behind her. "Hey! What'd you think of the game?"

Don't make a fool of yourself by turning around, she told herself, *you don't even know any boys, so he couldn't be talking to you*.

"Hello?" he called out again. Maybe he *was* talking to her. She cautiously turned around, trying to appear nonchalant.

"Uh . . . were you talking to me?" she finally stammered.

He looked amusedly around the gym, cocking one eyebrow up quizzically. It appeared they were the only two people in the gym. He answered slowly, "Evidently."

She shyly lowered her eyes. She couldn't keep from smiling. It *had* been a ridiculous question.

"Did you enjoy the game?"

She looked up and recognized Brett Collins, the guy every girl in school would give their eyeteeth to have looking at them like this.

The intensity of his gaze flustered her. In her nervousness, Janet forgot what the question was.

"I'm sorry. What did you ask me?"

"Did you enjoy the game?" he repeated, looking like he was doing his best to keep from outright laughter.

"Oh. Yes. It was . . . it was very good."

"And, what may I ask, was 'very good' about it? Was it good that we only lost by twenty points rather than thirty? Or was it . . . well why don't *you* tell me what was good about it?" he asked with a smile.

He was making fun of her now.

"Well . . . it was good . . . it was good to watch you play," she stuttered, her face turning ten shades of red. *What made her come up with such an absurd answer?*

"Wow! I'll take that as a compliment. So, the only thing 'good' about the game was watching *me* play? That goes a long way in making me feel better about losing an important game. If you promise to say more things like that, can I take you out for a soda? Would you mind waiting for me while I shower up and dress?"

"Uh, sure . . . I just need to tell my friends that I, um, will catch up with them later and . . ."

"I can drive you home."

"Oh. Actually I live kind of far out and . . ."

"I know where you live. Would it be okay with your parents if I gave you a ride?" he asked politely.

Her heart did a little flip. He *knew* where she ***lived***? She didn't even think he knew who she ***was*** much less where she ***lived.***

"That would be great." She gave him a dimpled smile and he thought he'd never seen anyone prettier.

"You sure you don't mind waiting?"

"Oh no, not at all," she assured him. *Why, she'd wait all night if he asked.*

And so began the most exciting year of her life.

Brett and Janet couldn't get enough of each other. She couldn't wait for school each morning. He carried her books as they walked hand in hand through the halls. Every girl envied how mesmerized he was with her.

Janet thought he was almost too good looking. He was over six feet, had dark hair that curled up at his nape where he grew it a little longer. He had broad shoulders and narrow hips and the most amazing green eyes she'd ever seen.

In the beginning she'd worried he'd be cocky and high on himself. How wrong she'd been! He never took himself too seriously. That was part of his appeal.

As for Brett, he'd never met anyone as enchantingly innocent and adorable as his Janet. She had no idea how stunning she was. She made him laugh easily with her naïveté and sense of humor.

The first time he'd seen her was in the school library. She was with a friend and they were laughing about something. She had a contagious laugh with the cutest dimple in her right cheek. He was trying to think of a reason to join them, but the librarian kicked them out before he got the chance.

After that, he started looking for her everywhere, asking questions about her. What was her name? Where did she live? Did she have a boyfriend? No one seemed to know much about her, except that she lived on a farm on the outskirts of town.

When he was heading to the locker room after the basketball game, he could hardly believe it was ***her*** sitting in the bleachers. He watched her for a few minutes. Watched her sitting there writing while everyone else filed out of the gym. Just when she'd finished gathering up her belongings and stood to leave, he'd called out to her. He'd been captivated ever since. He adored her. He adored everything about her.

The chemistry between them was wondrous. He was her first boyfriend, and it shocked her how strong the temptation was to do anything and everything. He would rest his hand on her knee and it was as if all her nerve endings were concentrated where his hand rested. She loved the touch of his strong, masculine hands. She loved combing her fingers through his hair, running her fingers down his jaw to his chin that had just a hint of a cleft.

Life was fun. Each day brought them closer and made drawing the line at kissing and cuddling more difficult. It was a temptation she brought nightly before God.

April 1959

One night as they were kissing good-bye, Brett lifted his head, took her face in his hands and stared into her eyes.

"What?" she asked, a little unnerved by how serious he looked.

"Do you know what Saturday is?" he spoke softly, his hands still cupped around her face.

"No, what is it?"

"We'll have been together a year. It's been a full year since I stopped you in the gym that night. I want to make it special. I planned a day just for us."

"How sweet!" She put her hands on his cheeks and pulled his mouth down to hers. Mmm, she loved the feel of his lips on hers.

He took her hands in his. "I hope you know how much you mean to me, Janet. How special I want this day to be. I'll pick you up at noon, dress casually and be ready to get spoiled."

Saturday came and she wore clam-diggers and a new blouse. She left her long, golden curls unclasped, just how he liked it best. She ran out as soon as he pulled up to the house. She was as excited as a little kid on Christmas morning.

At the end of their long driveway, he turned the opposite way from town.

"You do know the nearest town in this direction is at least an hour away, don't you?"

"Yup."

Now she was really curious about this very "special" day. She was sure he'd been planning a road trip up to Chicago, but he'd turned onto the road that took them deeper into the country.

As they drove, she teased him about his romanticism in wanting to celebrate this milestone. He put his arm around her and pulled her up against him. She fit into the crook of his arm perfectly, and she sighed in contentment. She would never forget the simple pleasure of riding in his car on this beautiful, warm spring day with the windows down and the pungent smell of lilacs filling the air.

Brett slowed the car and turned down a little dirt lane. Within minutes a picturesque little lake emerged. Willow branches softly skimmed the water that glistened under the sun's afternoon light. There was a clearing between some large trees and fresh spring grass made a soft carpet beneath them.

She gasped at the sight of the beautiful serenity, and the clear, sparkling water. How could she not have known about this place? Just like a kid, she bounded out of the car and ran down to the water to trail her fingers in it. She looked back to see if Brett was behind her, but he was busy getting things out of the trunk.

"The water feels great!" she called out delightedly. "You should have told me to wear my swimming suit so we could swim . . . you big silly."

He chuckled at her excitement. He knew she would respond just like this and he was inordinately pleased he knew her so well and could delight her so completely. He was carrying a huge picnic basket and a blanket. As he spread the blanket out onto the fresh grass, she almost bowled him over with a big hug.

"Thank you," she whispered, pressing herself against him and burying her nose in his thick neck and taking in the wonderful smell of him.

"You're welcome," he whispered back. "Let me show you all the goodies I packed for us."

He pulled her down on the blanket beside him and opened the basket, bringing out all sorts of delicious food—cheese, crackers, fresh fruit, sandwiches and even some homemade cookies for dessert. She stared at the bottle of wine he brought out last. She was surprised. They weren't legal to drink and her parents thought alcohol was from the devil himself. They would be crushed if they thought she was out here imbibing.

"Is that real wine?" she asked, still staring at the bottle.

His laughter at her innocence reflected such obvious amusement, she couldn't help but smile in return.

"But, you know I can't drink it."

"Why not? Wait . . ." He held his hand up to stop her, put his finger gently against her lips to silence her. "Don't answer, let me see if I know you well enough to answer for you. Okay, alcohol is a tool of the devil and taking a sip might turn you into an instant drunkard. Now, do I know you or what?" he grinned.

She couldn't help but laugh, he'd echoed her thoughts almost exactly. "Very funny! As a matter of fact, I wouldn't want to upset my parents because that is what *they* think about it."

"Well, it'll be our secret then, 'scout's honor.' And I promise, if you *do* become a drunk, I will refuse to feed your habit. Deal?"

"Deal." Janet surprised herself with her easy capitulation. How silly it would be to disappoint him over something as inconsequential as a few sips of wine anyway.

He invited her to sit back and relax. He would "wait" on her. He'd even thought to bring a transistor radio, and when he turned it on, Elvis

Presley was singing "Love Me Tender." She would remember this day as long as she lived, and every time she heard this song she would think of Brett and this magical day.

He poured some wine into two paper cups and handed her one.

"I have a toast."

"A toast? Who knew you could be this romantic? Is there no end to your charm?" she asked flirtatiously.

"I'm serious," he said, and suddenly he *looked* serious. He looked intently into her eyes and she smiled expectantly.

"I would like to propose a toast," he began, "to the most adorable, fun and desirable girl I've ever met, and to our future that promises to be filled with love, laughter and at least . . ." he paused, grinning.

"At least what?"

". . . at least six children." He tapped his cup against hers.

Brett's declaration of her desirability and the thought of having his babies made her catch her breath and instead of sipping the wine, she took a big gulp, her eyes never leaving his.

Golly she was beautiful! He was hardly able to think about anything but her. He was so captivated he could no longer envision a life that didn't include her.

"I take it you liked it?" he asked, looking pointedly down at her empty cup.

"I'm not sure I actually *liked* it, but I think it tasted better than I thought it would," she answered truthfully.

He refilled her cup. "Try sipping it this time," he suggested.

She took the cup dutifully and daintily sipped it as they munched on some of the fruit and talked about anything and everything. As always, their conversation was punctuated with lots of laughter. When the bottle was empty, he stood up and grabbed her hand, pulling her up.

"Let's go down to the water and put our feet in it."

Whoa. She felt dizzy as she stood up—could she be feeling the effects of a few cups of wine?

The water felt glorious! What a perfect day this was turning out to be. She wouldn't forget a single detail even if she lived to be a hundred.

She felt giddy with happiness. Being here with Brett, head over heels in love with him—did life get any better?

"The water feels so good. You really should have told me to wear my swimming suit," she gently rebuked him.

"If I would have asked you to wear your swimming suit, it would have ruined the surprise," he grinned. "But . . . there's always the possibility of swimming in our birthday suits," he playfully added.

"Birthday suits?"

He laughed. "You know . . . the outfits we had on when we were born?"

As understanding dawned, she flushed a deep pink and looked down at her feet in the water.

"How about it? Shall we give it a try? I promise not to look until you're in the water and we'll just stay underwater. We can pretend we *do* have our swim suits on."

Was he serious? Janet wondered how she could even be considering it. Was it the wine or the magical, romantic perfection of the entire day? It *did* sound exciting! What would it hurt? No one would ever know. It wasn't as if she'd be strutting around naked or anything.

"Do you *promise* not to look until I'm completely underwater?" she asked seriously.

"I give you my solemn word," he quickly answered. He could hardly believe she was going to do this. "I'll stand behind that tree over there and not take my eyes off the horizon until you tell me I can," he assured her.

"Okay. I promise not to look at you either." As if he cared.

After they were both in the water, they laughingly splashed around, relishing the feel of the water on their naked bodies. It heightened every desire they'd ever experienced for each other. She swam close to him and impulsively splashed water in his face.

She laughed at his surprised expression.

"Hey! What'd I do to deserve that?"

"I couldn't resist," she laughed.

"Well, if you do it again, I'm going to give you a dunking you won't forget!" he teasingly warned.

"No you won't, because you gave me your 'solemn word' not to touch me, remember?" she taunted.

"Just try it, because I don't remember promising you I wouldn't *touch . . .*"

He wasn't able to finish his sentence due to the big wave of water splashed in his face.

With a lightning quick response, his strong hand encircled her wrist and he pulled her against him. The feel of their naked bodies pressed against each other was breathtaking.

Their kiss was violent in its intensity. She could taste the wine in his mouth. He'd never felt anything as glorious as her warm wet body pressed against his. He picked her up as if she were no heavier than a doll, trudged slowly out of the water and laid her gently on the blanket. He hungrily took in her beautiful body. All thoughts of keeping his hands off of her left him. He groaned aloud as he gave up the fight to resist.

As for her, all thoughts of modesty, purity and goodness were gone. Instead, she marveled at the sight of his taut body. The water made his thick eyelashes stand out in dark spikes. She sighed at the exquisite pleasure his hands on her body were giving her. She wanted every part of him to touch every part of her. The potency of their shared desire took them down a path of no return.

"We should stop," he whispered huskily.

"No . . . please . . . not yet," she whispered. She wasn't ready for it to end. She felt a small stab of pain, but it was fleeting. She involuntarily moaned in pleasure.

He collapsed against her, then rolled over to his side and pulled her against him, her body spooning perfectly into his.

With his lips pressed gently against her still damp hair he whispered, "I will always love you Janet. You know that don't you? I don't want to ever lose you. I can't bear the thought of life without you."

"I love you, too," she whispered so softly he could barely hear her.

As she lay contentedly tucked against his body, sanity slowly returned. The sinking realization of what they'd done overwhelmed her. How could she have let it happen? How could she be lying here in broad daylight without a stitch of clothing on? She suddenly felt shy, acutely aware of her nudity. Brett felt her stiffening and watched her attempt to curl up tighter to shield herself from his eyes. Sensitive to the change, he asked her if she'd like him to grab her clothes.

"Please," she answered, without turning to look at him.

As soon as he got up, Janet pulled the blanket up to cover herself. She tried not to stare at his naked physique as he walked away. Evidently, he wasn't experiencing the same modesty she was. He slowly pulled on his own clothes before gathering hers.

He brought them to her and dutifully walked back behind the tree and stared at the horizon. She scrambled quickly into her clothes and then called out to him. He walked back and pulled her into his arms, holding her tightly against him. She buried her head in his neck and started crying.

He pulled his head back to look at her. *Why was she crying?*

"What's wrong? Please don't cry. Look at me," he implored.

She shook her head mutely, refusing to look up at him. She wiped her nose with her hand.

"We should go."

"But we haven't eaten! Aren't you hungry?"

She shook her head.

"Eat just a few bites, it'll make you feel better. Honest, I make a pretty 'mean' sandwich," he tried to lighten up the mood.

"I'll try," she responded woodenly.

She felt like she was chewing cardboard. She forced herself to swallow and almost gagged.

"Come on," Brett teased, "it can't be that bad!"

"I'm sorry. But I'm really not hungry. I think the wine made me feel a little sick, my mouth feels dry and . . ."

"Janet, this isn't what I wanted. Let's just relax a minute." He was feeling desperate to get her out of her despondent mood and back to the playfulness she'd exhibited earlier. What had he done? He should have known better, he should have shown more restraint. He knew how important her purity was to her. He felt like a selfish cad, no better than an animal.

He took a strand of her hair and tucked it behind her ear. He took his finger and tilted up her chin to look at him. "Please, Janet. I can't stand to see you sad. You know I didn't plan for this to happen don't you? I'm really, truly sorry. Will you forgive me?"

"You can't take all the blame," she said softly. "If anything, I'm *more* to blame." She blushed, remembering how she'd practically begged him *not* to stop. "I don't know what's wrong with me," she said dejectedly.

"There's nothing 'wrong' with you! We're two people in love, it's natural to want as much physical intimacy as possible—there'd be something 'wrong' with us if we *didn't* want each other."

"But God forbids it. He won't bless us now. We'll be punished. 'He chastens those He loves . . .'" she moaned, remembering some of the Bible verses she'd heard all her life.

"Surely your God forgives, doesn't He?" Brett questioned. He couldn't help but think of his "devout" philandering father. He certainly hadn't experienced any "chastening" for *his* escapades.

"Yes, He forgives . . . but I don't know. I just know He punishes too. And now I've ruined it. I've messed up," she muttered as fresh tears filled her eyes.

"You haven't 'messed' up. Please, Janet. *Please.* It's going to be alright. I *promise* not to let it happen again. I love you, and want nothing more than for you to be happy." He was desperate to lighten her mood.

She continued to sit stiffly on the blanket, staring at the ground.

Brett didn't take his eyes off her face. When a tear started rolling down her cheek, he reached over and gently wiped it away.

"What is it? What's going through your mind right now? Tell me. I want to try and understand so I can make it better."

"You can't make it better. Nothing can make it better. It's a done deed." She shook her head dejectedly, tears continuing to fall.

He quietly suggested that perhaps they should head back, so as not to worry her parents.

The mention of her parents brought a fresh stab of guilt. They would be horrified by her behavior! She never dreamed she'd fall prey to this uncontrollable hunger for a man who wasn't her husband. It had been driven into her as long as she could remember that *this* was an act to be shared *only* by husband and wife. Now she would never know the wondrous gift God had wanted to give her. Her wedding night wouldn't be the spectacular union God had planned. She was filled with guilt and remorse.

They silently packed everything back in the car. She didn't say a word as they drove, just stared out the window. Brett tried to make her smile or talk, but she was so unresponsive he finally gave up. What a switch this ride was from the one that began their day. He was frustrated and feeling sick about what happened. He was helpless to remedy it, and terrified he'd done something that might cause him to lose her. Surely she didn't think he *planned* for it to happen?

He was remorseful about his lack of restraint and conscience stricken he had taken advantage of her.

"Please talk to me," he pleaded one more time. He placed his warm hand over hers, but she let her hand lay motionless beneath it.

When they pulled up to her house, she jumped out of the car, thanked him politely for "everything" and walked woodenly up to her house. She hadn't waited for him to open the door for her or even given him a kiss good-bye.

"Hey!" Brett called out. He was exasperated with his failure to reach her. He didn't want to leave with this sick feeling in the pit of his stomach.

"Would you like me to come to church with you tomorrow?"

Surely this would soften her! She'd asked him many times to go to church with her, but he'd never agreed to go.

She stopped and turned around, staring at him blankly. "Church?" she questioned, as if it was a new word to her or something. "Oh. No thanks. I don't think . . . I don't think I'll be going tomorrow. Thanks anyway though." She gave him a tight smile and a little wave before turning away.

Church was the *last* place she wanted to be tomorrow, Janet thought. She had no desire to be around all those good people. She was sure they'd be able to see right through her and see exactly what she'd done.

Brett sat in his car a long time. He watched her let herself into the house, willing her to look back and at least give him a smile, but she never did. He finally started his car and drove slowly away. He was hurt by how short and formal she was in her goodbye. He'd tried so hard to make the day special. *Damn!* What had he done? He needed her. Surely she couldn't think what happened could do anything but increase his love for her. Hadn't he convinced her of that?

Janet desperately wanted to avoid any conversation with her parents. What she had done would probably be as obvious to them as the nose on her face. She could just imagine them asking her if she'd enjoyed their "special day." *Oh it was wonderful,* she'd say. *You'd be so proud of your self-controlled, modest, lady-like little girl. Please God, let them not be home. Please don't let anything come of what I've done. I promise not to let it happen again—just please, let it be okay.*

The house was empty. A note had been left on the kitchen table. They had gone to take dinner to an ailing church member and would not be home until later in the evening. Perfect. She would make sure she was in bed and "fast asleep" when they returned.

Janet wasn't herself at school the following Monday. Her friends were eager to hear all about Janet and Brett's mystery date. They were disappointed and more than a little curious when all she shared was that it had been "nice." *Nice?* An entire day planned especially for her with the gorgeous Brett Collins, and all she would say about it was that it was "nice?" Something was awry, but despite their persistent prodding, Janet wasn't sharing.

Brett was stumped by the change in her. He couldn't begin to understand why she remained so distraught. He made every attempt to restore their old camaraderie. Yet she was prickly, constantly taking things the wrong way.

She'd never been insecure or doubtful about the genuineness of his feelings for her. Now she demanded to know how he spent every minute away from her. It was starting to drive him crazy. He loved her, didn't she get that? If anything, he was more crazy about her than before. He told her if he wasn't who he claimed to be, if he *really* couldn't be trusted, she'd be better off without him. But the fact was, he was *exactly* who he claimed to be. He loved her and would never do *anything* to hurt her. All this doubt and suspicion was wasting time that should be spent enjoying what they had together.

Before that fateful Saturday she *had* been confident in Brett's adoration. Nothing had weighed on her conscience then. If only she could go back in time and change a few minor details. Brett was bending over backwards trying to get her out of her self-imposed slump. He'd bristled at some of her probing questions. She was absurdly hurt at his irritation because she knew he had every right to *be* irritated. She knew she was being unreasonable.

Janet was terrified she'd lost Brett's respect by so easily allowing him to know her in the most intimate way possible. She was afraid she was turning him away with her suspicion and immaturity. She wasn't even acting likable, much less lovable.

Before their escapade, Janet hadn't cared about any of his previous girlfriends. Now, there were things she wanted to know. Had he been as intimate with them? Had he ever taken anyone else to that same spot? Had he lost respect and become disinterested in them after he got what he wanted?

Janet came out of one of her classes one day and spotted Brett talking to Marilyn, one of his old girlfriends. Marilyn saw Janet watching them and deliberately put her hand on his arm. *What was that all about?*

Brett turned around just then and gave her his usual big grin, always happy to see her. He immediately recognized Janet was perturbed about something. He quickly ended his conversation and strolled over to her.

Janet willed herself not to care, or at the very least, not to *show* she cared. She forced a smile as he approached.

Brett sensed her coolness and wondered what he'd done *now*. Surely she wasn't bothered just because he'd been talking to Marilyn? Maybe some straight talk would clear the air.

He put a hand on each of her shoulders, turning her so they were face to face.

"Janet. Please tell me what I can do to get you to act like your old self. I miss the old Janet. You must know you're the only girl for me. I've never loved anyone the way I love you and never will." He stared resolutely into her eyes until he could see her softening toward him.

"I'm sorry," she laid her head against his chest. "I don't know what's wrong with me. I know I'm acting beastly, yet I can't seem to help myself."

He twined his fingers in her hair and held her against him.

"You needn't be sorry, Janet. I just want you to be your old self. C'mon now, I need you to think like I do. We're made for each other. We're going to spend the rest of our lives together. Grow old together."

She smiled in response, but still couldn't shake the awful feeling that things were never going to be the same.

Their desire for each other certainly hadn't abated. She knew how difficult it was for him to restrain himself, but he stayed true to his word. She trusted him to never let it happen again. Shamefully, she wanted more of what she'd experienced that day, she couldn't look at his hands without remembering how they'd made her feel that day. How had he known just where and how to touch her? Was it from experience? The thought of his hands making another girl feel what she'd felt was like a knife in her heart.

Maybe that was part of what was making her feel so jealous of Marilyn. She couldn't help comparing herself to her. Marilyn was petite and perfect. All the guys thought so. She was slender yet had been lucky enough to be well endowed as well. She wore beautiful cashmere sweater sets, worn so tight the buttons looked on the verge of popping off any moment.

Janet couldn't help but compare her own small breasts to hers. Brett must feel like he's hugging a boy compared to her. Janet was tall. She'd always wished she was just a few inches shorter, just enough so that when she wore stylish pumps she wouldn't be taller than most boys. Heavens! She felt like a goon next to Marilyn's petite perfection. But Brett was tall himself. When he held her close she couldn't imagine wanting to be any shorter. He often told her how he loved her height. Still though, sometimes Janet could get so carried away thinking how much sexier and more desirable Marilyn was, she'd have herself convinced it was only a matter of time before Brett realized how irresistible she was and go back to her. She'd torture herself with images of them enjoying the same intimacy they'd shared. Maybe he was just waiting for an excuse to end it, and Lord knew, she was giving him one.

She resolved to pull herself together and trust Brett. His behavior matched his words; she had no reason do doubt his feelings for her were genuine. She would enjoy every minute she had with him. Whether or not it was forever, he wanted to be with her *now.* She needed to quit acting like an immature child and enjoy the *here* and *now.* Whether or not she thought Marilyn would make a sexier, more desirable girlfriend, the fact remained—Brett had chosen *her.*

Even though she knew what they'd done was wrong she'd been unable to resist playing "Love Me Tender" on her record player almost every night and reliving every minute of their day together.

About six weeks after their rendezvous at the lake, Janet woke up feeling queasy. For the last week or so she'd been having cramps and kept thinking she was about to have her period. She'd feel better in the afternoon, but the following morning the queasiness returned. Janet tried to convince herself it was just a wacky bug, but deep down she knew better. She struggled internally. She couldn't help but feel a rush of awe and wonderment that a new life had been created, yet under her dire circumstances, it felt more like the chastening she had so desperately hoped to escape.

The thought of telling her parents something that would bring their world crashing down around them made her literally want to die. Each day the hopelessness of her situation and the inevitable truth that would soon be evident made her withdraw more and more into herself.

She was reluctant to say anything to Brett because she knew he'd insist on marrying her. He would think it was their only option, the *right* thing to do. But that would mean his plans for college would be ruined. He'd received a scholarship to attend the University of Michigan where he planned to get his medical degree. He was determined to be successful, to escape the poverty he'd grown up in. How could she take that dream from him? If they were meant to last, they would. He would be leaving for school in a few short months, surely she could hide it from him that long? She figured the baby would be born early to mid-January. Could she go away somewhere? Supposedly to visit relatives, have the baby and return before Easter break? Would she really be able to give up their baby for adoption? To keep that secret from him the rest of her life? Well, she didn't have a choice. Any solution that kept Brett out of her life was inconceivable, heartbreaking. Yet any solution that took his dream away from him wasn't acceptable either.

She was living a lie at home. She wasn't the girl her parents thought she was. Her regret and self-incrimination kept her from enjoying the carefree, loving relationship she'd always had with them.

When she first realized she was pregnant she had pled with God to give her another chance. Let it be a nightmare she could wake up from, having learned her lesson. But it was real, and she couldn't delay telling her parents any longer. She resolved to tell them that night at dinner.

Her father finished the blessing on their food ". . . and our bodies to Thy service. Amen."

After the prayer, Janet kept her head down. Tears welled in her eyes as she tried to muster up the courage to tell them she was pregnant.

"Janet? Is everything all right?" her mother asked softly.

Janet shook her head mutely. Tears fell onto the empty plate in front of her.

"I've done something awful." Janet's voice was wobbly. "I'm not sure you're going to be able to forgive me."

Maggie's heart constricted, dreading what Janet had to share with them. She and Don had had suspicions about Janet's "illness." They so desperately didn't want to believe it. Pleaded with God to let it not be so. Prayed that if their suspicions were right, the good Lord would show them how to deal with it. Maggie blamed herself for not talking more about what temptations Janet might be battling and for allowing her too much freedom with Brett.

"Honey, surely you know you couldn't do *anything* we couldn't forgive you for?"

"I don't know, Mama. This is pretty big. I've really, really gotten myself into a mess and . . ." Janet gulped back a sob. "You've been so wonderful to me . . . and I've failed you in the worst possible way."

Maggie reached for Janet's hand. "Look at me Janet."

Janet finally lifted her tear-stained face and looked at her mother. There were tears in her mother's eyes as well.

Janet took a deep, shaky breath before blurting out, "I'm pregnant, Mama. Hurting you and Daddy is what hurts the most. But I don't know what to do." Janet collapsed into great gulping sobs, "I don't know what to ***do***."

Maggie knelt and wrapped her arms around Janet.

"Sh, sh, honey. The Lord knows all about it. This baby isn't a surprise to Him. Somehow He'll work it out. You'll see, it'll be alright." She closed her eyes tightly, wishing for all the world that it *would* be alright, that they *could* fix it for her. "Daddy and I are probably partly to blame . . ."

"No Mama! Don't ever think that. You've showered me with love. You taught me right from wrong. You brought me up to do things God's way and I went my own way . . . and now . . . now I won't ever have His blessing."

"Honey, there's not a one of us without sin. Christ took that sin upon Himself and because of that we can confess our sins and be cleansed from all unrighteousness. You know those verses." Maggie cupped Janet's face, making her look her in the eye. "***But*** that does not mean it's gonna be easy; that this isn't God's perfect plan for you. All we can do now is put it in His hands and trust Him to show us the way."

Janet hadn't been able to bring herself to look at her father. She didn't want to see his disappointment in her in his eyes. He silently slipped up behind her, offering her a tissue to blow her nose and dab at her tears. She mumbled a thanks, but still didn't look up at him. But if she had, she would have seen the tears in his eyes as well. He knew the days ahead would be much harder than Janet could imagine. She wouldn't come through it unscathed regardless of what she ended up deciding to do. He felt an enormous weight on his chest for his precious daughter, his little girl that meant the world to him. There was no sense in playing the coulda, woulda, shoulda game. It had happened. Now they needed to figure out how to deal with it.

He knelt down in front of her, too, "Sweetheart, surely you know there's *nothing* in the world you could do to make us stop loving you? We hurt because *you* hurt."

How could Janet have doubted their devotion to her? Not even *this*, what must be the most devastating thing she could ever do to them, made them reject her. Janet turned towards her father and lay her head against his chest, "Oh, Daddy," she sniffled. "I'm so, so sorry . . ." She clung to him and sobbed until she didn't have any tears left.

When she finally stopped crying, her father asked, "What does Brett say? I'm surprised he didn't insist on being here with you when you told us."

"He doesn't know. I don't want him to know. I thought maybe I could go away, have the baby, give it up for adoption and come back. I can't let him give up his dream."

Her parents looked at each other, both thinking the same thing—her love for Brett *must* be genuine, because she was putting his dreams above her own. They knew *her* dream would be to marry him and have his baby, but she knew she would always regret taking away his dream. She didn't want to live the rest of her life knowing she made him give that up.

~ ~

Summer was in full swing and Janet still hadn't decided how she was going to hide her pregnancy from Brett after he went away to school in the fall. He was planning on coming home for Christmas when she would be in the final weeks of her pregnancy. She'd have to fabricate a story about needing to visit out of state relatives. It would be heart-breaking not to see him at Christmas time, but it was the only answer. She was almost four months along. It was a wonder she wasn't showing. Ironically, her breasts were fuller, but other than that her body hadn't changed much.

Brett had a summer job at the Five and Dime in town. Sometimes Janet would pop in and spend his lunch break with him. He loved it when she surprised him, said it always made his day.

It was a beautiful, sunny August day. He would be happy to see her, they would undoubtedly talk about how hard it was going to be, not seeing each other for three whole months. She would wait to tell him she wouldn't be home for Christmas until the last minute. Otherwise she feared he'd find a way to come home before then. She couldn't imagine him being willing to wait until Easter to see her. Janet hated the thought of not seeing him all those months, too. It would be difficult, but it was the only solution she could come up with.

After coming in from the bright sunlight, it took a minute for Janet's eyes to adjust to the interior of the store. She didn't find Brett in his usual spot at the counter, so she strolled around looking for him.

She rounded a corner and her breath caught painfully in her chest. Brett was holding Marilyn tightly against him. He had his head bent down to hers and he was rubbing her back.

Tears welled in Janet's eyes. *You fool, Janet! You've been so stupid! Why didn't you listen to your gut? You knew all along it was too good to last. Did you really think he would want **you** when it was obvious **she** still wanted him?*

They hadn't seen her and she crept quietly out of the store and then started running when she got out on the street. She didn't want anyone to see her. She ducked into a phone booth, dug desperately through her purse for a dime and called her parents.

Alarmed at how hysterical she sounded, they promised to come get her right away.

Oh, how it hurt! It hurt worse than anything she'd ever felt before. She understood now why it was called heartbroken. Her heart felt like it was being squeezed so hard it might cut off her very breath. No worries *now* about keeping Brett away. She *never* wanted to see him again. She was doubly glad she had kept her pregnancy a secret. She would never want to be married to a man who wanted someone other than her.

She would need her parents help in making sure he never found her. Since his feelings had obviously changed, he would probably be relieved not to have to break it off with her face to face. Janet would be doing him a favor.

Brett was worried about Janet. She often stopped by to see him at work, but he hadn't heard from her all day. He tried calling her house several times but no one picked up. As soon as his shift ended, he drove straight to her house. It wasn't like her to be incommunicado.

When he pulled up to her house, he half expected her to be on the porch waiting for him, but Janet wasn't in sight and there weren't any lights on. Where could they all have gone at this time of night? He knocked loudly and persistently; if anyone was there they would have to acknowledge him. After a while, he dejectedly got back in his car and headed home.

Something wasn't right. He felt a nagging fear that he was losing her. It had all started that day at the lake. Things hadn't been the same since. Yet lately, he'd thought things were getting better. Surely he'd proved to her that he *could* control himself, hadn't he?

What had happened, happened. He couldn't undo it. He knew she was a good, religious girl, he *knew* better than to go that far with her, but he hadn't bargained on the magnitude of *her* response to *him.* It was her *matched* passion that proved too much for him.

He hated witnessing her devastating guilt. He was determined to make it right. He would never give up trying to convince her they belonged together, not now. Not ever.

Maggie had been looking into places where Janet could go and have her baby. After the birth, Janet could return and finish up her last year of high school. She could pick up her life just as if it'd never happened. No one would have to know.

Maggie thought she'd found the perfect place in a little town about nine hours south of them, tucked into the beautiful Smoky Mountains. A place called The Haven. They were reportedly very discreet and offered complete privacy. A single woman named Eva Mayes had built it. She housed the girls and arranged for the adoptions as well. It sounded ideal.

Eva Mayes was a devout Christian woman who'd seen the need to provide a safe haven for girls who found themselves "in trouble." Though she never married, her father had left her a considerable inheritance that ensured she would never have to work.

In Eva's search to find purpose and fulfillment, she came up with the idea to build a large home to house these hopeless, pitiful young girls. So, The Haven was built and Eva made it a safe and loving home for girls to come to in the early months of their pregnancy and receive care right through their delivery.

Eva taught the girls Bible verses that revealed God's great love for them. She convinced them nothing they could ever do could make God love them any less. She implored them to trust Him as their Savior and claim His promise that He'd make all things work for good for those who loved Him and were called according to His purpose. It was up to them whether they would be defined by their past or their possibilities.

The joy Eva felt when she matched childless couples with her precious babies was incalculable. She did thorough interviews of all the couples that came to her. She refused to allow a single one of these little ones be adopted into a family that didn't share her faith in the Lord.

Janet and her parents drove down to the The Haven the day after Janet's agitated sighting of Brett with Marilyn. They fell in love with the place and decided there was no reason Janet couldn't begin her stay there that day. That would ensure she wouldn't have to confront Brett.

Her parents promised to guard her secret about the baby. They would think of *something* to tell Brett. Maybe they'd say that she'd gone to visit a relative, that she hadn't had the courage to tell him face to face her feelings for him had changed. Janet insisted he'd be more relieved than hurt. After all, it would spare *him* having to tell her about his renewed feelings for Marilyn.

From the first day Eva met Janet, Eva knew she was special. She loved all her "girls," as she fondly called them, every one of them had a special place in her heart. But Janet was unique. Eva grew very close to her and would miss her sweet, gentle spirit and quiet intelligence.

They often talked long into the night. Their conversations spanned all sorts of topics: books they'd read, current events and interesting people and places.

Eva was forever trying to convince Janet God had allowed what happened for a reason, perhaps for a multitude of reasons. She said being able to give a couple God's most precious creation when their hope had all but disappeared was indescribably wondrous. Janet would see.

Still, Eva worried Janet was growing too attached to her unborn baby. The way she smiled when she felt the baby move, touching her stomach in wonder. The way she'd laughingly comment, "You're a busy little thing, aren't you? I bet your parents won't be getting much . . ." She stopped mid-sentence, unable to admit aloud she and the baby would soon be separated.

Eva had left The Haven for a night to attend her Aunt's funeral. She knew she'd done the right thing, but now she was eager to return to her girls. As Eva drove through the last few minutes of daylight, her thoughts were drawn to Janet. She had weighed heavily on Eva's mind these past few weeks. She was going to miss her more than she wanted to admit. She could hardly believe her time was nearing.

Eva pulled into the driveway, thinking longingly of putting her feet up and enjoying a hot cup of tea. It had been a long drive back from her cousin's home. Because she was anxious to get home, she had resolutely gotten up before dawn and driven straight through. As she wearily gathered her things from the trunk, one of the girls came out to meet her.

She started to greet her, but was silenced by the solemn look on Sue Ann's face.

"I been waitin' for you," Sue Ann began worriedly. "Janet started havin' the pains last night, and we haven't heard nuthin. She had to have that baby by now . . . don't ya think?" She twisted her nightgown in her hands, waiting plaintively for Eva to answer.

Eva's heart jumped. It was too early. Shoot. She hadn't wanted Janet to be alone.

"Did anyone go with her?"

"No, Ma'am. Janet called the nurse and when she got here, she said they's prolly not the real thing. Just the fake ones that come first. But they started gettin' worse, so she took her to the hospital. She said it's too early. No one called, and she never came back and we's worried . . ."

Eva took Sue Ann's hand and told her not to worry, she'd go up to the hospital right away and find out how Janet was doing. Everything would be fine.

"No news is good news, isn't that what they say?" Eva convinced Sue Ann to go back into the house; she'd be back soon.

Eva's weariness was forgotten as she climbed back in her car. She had an anxious premonition that things were going awry. Her adrenaline kicked in. She prayed for Janet and her baby on the short drive to the hospital.

She bounded up the short flight of stairs to the reception area. The receptionist was doing her best not to nod off and Eva's sudden appearance startled her. Embarrassed to be found in a less than an alert mode, she nervously fumbled around finding Janet's information. Eva couldn't stop herself from impatiently drumming her fingers on the desk, making the poor woman even less competent.

When Eva finally got what precious little information the receptionist was able to give her, she forced herself to walk slowly and quietly. She did not want to wake Janet if she was sleeping. She prayed there was someone on the floor who could give her details.

Thankfully, the doctor had been called back to the hospital for another birth and was able to give her all the pertinent details of Janet's labor, the shock of the twins, and the fact that Janet didn't know she'd had two babies.

Eva stood wordlessly in front of the doctor as he spoke. She hardly knew what to think. It was all so unsettling. Eva found it disturbing that Janet thought she'd only delivered one child and it was especially distressing that she had been insistent about *keeping* the baby.

She mumbled something to the doctor about needing time by herself to think and pray. After some contemplation and fervent prayer for wisdom, she finally felt ready to see Janet.

Appallingly enough, she felt allowing Janet to continue to believe she'd only given birth to one baby *was* the best answer. She knew instinctively it would be doubly hard on Janet to give up twins.

The problem now was the couple she'd chosen for Janet's baby could not afford two, yet how could she even *consider* splitting up the girls?

There were two couples Eva knew would make perfect parents for Janet's baby. She had been torn between the two, prayed over it for weeks.

Ultimately she chose the Ryans. Though they struggled financially, she knew they were rich spiritually—and wasn't that the most important thing? They were ecstatic when Eva called and announced their long awaited baby would be arriving in less than a month.

The other couple, the Davidsons, could certainly afford two, yet her heart ached at the thought of disappointing the Ryans this late in the game. *Please, Lord, give me direction.* Would it really be so wrong to split the girls up and bless *two* families?

She whispered one more prayer before opening the door to Janet's room. The poor dear was sleeping soundly. What an undeniably beautiful girl she was! Her cheeks still had the fullness of youth. Why, she looked no more than thirteen years old. Janet had no inkling of her own beauty. Her long lashes fanned over the dark smudges under her eyes. Her honey-gold curls lay tangled across the pillow. She looked paler than normal, making the handful of freckles strewn across her slightly turned up nose stand out more than usual.

Oh, how Eva was going to miss her! She had become like a daughter really. She had such a sweet, sweet way about her. Because of Janet's level headedness and strong faith, Eva had found it difficult to understand how Janet had allowed the physical intimacy that resulted in her pregnancy.

Janet never shared anything about the father of her baby, but Eva knew she still cherished his memory in her heart. The only time Eva dared bring him up, Janet looked down, refusing to talk about him. Eva remembered looking at her closely, watching the play of emotions on her face. She was sure Janet still had feelings for the boy.

It saddened Eva that Janet had endured the delivery all on her own. She quietly pulled a chair over to Janet's bedside. She would let the sweet child rest as long she could. As Eva sat watching Janet's even breathing, she drifted off herself.

Janet felt disoriented when she opened her eyes. Where was she? The realization and remembrance of all she'd been through made her chest tighten anxiously.

She sighed and heard soft snoring next to her. She felt a rush of grateful relief to see Eva right there beside her, sleeping.

"Eva!" she whispered.

"Eva!" she whispered again, this time more urgently. Eva opened her eyes, looking a little out of it herself.

"Oh, Eva, thank God you're here! It's been terrible. They wouldn't even let me hold her . . ." she spoke haltingly, her voice choked with emotion. "You've *got* to get her for me, they'll listen to you. I'm sorry, I'm *really* sorry, about having to go back on my word, but I couldn't live with myself if I let a stranger raise her." Tears rolled down her cheeks as she stared imploringly at Eva.

Eva got up and sat on the edge of Janet's bed. She impulsively pulled her into her chest, hugging her tightly. Eva continued to hold her close, not wanting Janet to see the tears in her own eyes. She struggled to find words to comfort her.

"Sh, sh, love . . . it'll be alright. I promise. It'll get better. You'll realize soon enough you made the right decision. It's a selfless decision. It's all about those . . . er, the baby. Just think about the baby, love. Just think about her. I've told you so much about the Ryans. Please trust me," she pulled back so she could look Janet in the eyes.

She needed Janet to calm down. She couldn't reason with her in this state. She sent up a silent prayer for the right words to calm her and convince her she was doing the right thing. She reiterated what a noble, unselfish decision it was. It was really the *only* choice Janet had. Didn't she see?

Janet slowly got control of her emotions and closed her eyes, sighing in defeat. Eva had been her last hope, and now it was obvious she wasn't going to help her either. She felt betrayed. Betrayed by everyone claiming to love her.

Apparently, Janet's personal happiness didn't matter. Nothing she could say would convince them to let her keep her baby. Janet was more than emotionally spent at trying.

The last twenty-four hours had been an emotional roller coaster. Terrified something was wrong because the baby was coming too early.

Way up with elation at having a healthy baby. Way down in a frantic panic when they wouldn't even let her hold her. Desolate when she realized even her parents were not going to side with her. But through it all she'd retained a tiny sliver of hope that Eva might side with her. Now she was plunged back into the depths with the realization that no, Eva wouldn't side with her either.

Without opening her eyes, Janet asked to be left alone. As much as Eva hated to leave her, she knew she was too exhausted to be of much help; she was emotionally spent as well. She knew Janet wouldn't be at peace until she came to accept it on her own, in her own way. The poor thing was strong in ways that surprised them all. Eva was confident Janet would be able to reconcile in her heart and mind she was making the ultimate sacrifice for her daughter. The *right* decision.

Eva let herself silently into the large home that housed her girls, tiptoed to her room and closed the door. She had an attached study where she kept her beloved books and files on couples vying for her precious babies.

She sat heavily onto the big, comfortable chair that was her refuge when she needed to get away to think and pray. She sighed and pressed her index fingers against each temple, feeling a tension headache coming on.

As soon as Eva had met Bill and Jean Ryan she knew they'd be perfect parents for Janet's baby. Their deep devotion and commitment to God and each other was evident from the moment she met them and she was confident that Janet's baby would thrive in their home.

The Ryans had met at church and dated right through high school. Jean's only dream was to be a wife and mother. She'd always pictured herself with a house full of children. After years and years of trying to conceive, the deep disappointment and slow dissolution of their dreams almost destroyed their marriage.

Jean felt diminished as a woman, and Bill felt helpless trying to convince her having each other was enough. They internalized their pain, not finding solace in each other's arms like they always had. It didn't help matters that they constantly struggled to make ends meet. Jean often thought they wouldn't have been able to afford a house full of children anyway.

They became more involved in church, concentrated on serving each other and others. It had been a long road to reconciliation and acceptance, but together they got there.

When the Ryan's entered their thirties, they decided the only way they were going to experience parenthood was through adoption. A friend from church told them about The Haven. When they contacted The Haven they were told the proprietor wanted to meet with them in person. They were as impressed with Eva as she had been with them. They returned home with joyful expectation that God was going to bless them with a baby to adopt.

When the news reached them about their baby's impending birth, they were jubilant. Just days from now, they would be bringing their baby home!

Eva remembered the Ryans' exuberance when they heard the news, but they had only prepared for one baby and Eva knew with certainty they could not afford two—*yet, how could she disappoint them **now**?*

She brought her hands together in a steeple under her chin. *Lord, what should I do?* The thought of splitting up sisters seemed cruel, yet God wanted to grant His children the desires of their hearts. Would it be so awful to bless *two* couples with the deep desires of their hearts?

Eva sighed tiredly, stood up and looked around her small study. When her eyes lit upon her file cabinet of potential parents, she walked over and pulled out the file on the Davidsons. She scanned over the pertinent details, noting how much closer they lived than the Ryans. The Ryans lived in rural upstate New York, a two-day drive. As soon as the they heard Janet was in labor they'd set off. They would be here by morning.

The Davidsons lived in the suburbs of Cincinnati, they could be here in less than four hours. Unlike the Ryans, they could easily afford the burden of two babies. She was sure they would welcome two. Yet, *still* the idea of disappointing the Ryan's was abhorrent.

If only she could discuss it with Janet. But she knew that was out of the question. Janet was an emotional wreck right now. She'd been so mature about it all, it was easy to forget she was only seventeen years old. Almost a baby herself.

Eva had told Janet all about the Ryans. Janet had looked forward to meeting them. Eva always encouraged her girls to meet the adoptive parents, seeing the love, joy and gratitude on their faces confirmed in their hearts they were doing the right thing.

Eva walked back to her chair with the file in her hands. She resignedly sat back down, reading the notes she'd made about them.

Kate Davidson miscarried during her first pregnancy and complications from it had necessitated a full hysterectomy. Instead of sinking into despair, as many young couples might have, they trusted that God had a different plan for them. Yes, Eva had been very, very impressed with this young couple. God had blessed them materially, and they were willing to take as many babies as Eva could send their way.

Eva spent a considerable amount of time on her knees that morning, pleading with God to give her a clear answer to her dilemma. As she dressed, the thought occurred to her that perhaps if she met with the Davidsons face to face, she might gain more insight as to what she should do.

When the Davidsons got the call from Eva, they couldn't help but hope it meant a baby was on the way for them. They excitedly made arrangements to leave within the hour.

~ ~

When Eva met them at the door, the expectant looks on their faces made her feel guilty for possibly bringing them here with false hopes.

She was truthful, telling them about the misgivings she was experiencing, about how the couple she'd chosen for Janet's baby could not afford two babies, yet how desperately she didn't want to let them down.

They were en route even as they spoke. She guiltily explained that Janet didn't even know she'd had twins, and *why* she didn't.

Kate and John looked at each other—could they dare hope one or both of these baby girls might be theirs? Eva observed their shared look of hope, looked at their hands clutched between them and made up her mind.

"Would you be ready to take a baby girl home with you?"

"Oh, yes!" they answered in unison, smiling at their shared response.

Under normal circumstances, the adoptive parents met each of her girls. She was deeply disappointed the Davidsons would not be meeting Janet. She spoke of Janet affectionately, wanting them to understand what a truly wonderful girl had brought their baby into this world.

Kate's eyes filled with tears as Eva talked about the difficulty Janet was experiencing about letting go of her baby. Kate's heart ached for this young girl, bearing all this on her own and being forced to give up the life she'd carried all these months.

Kate stood up and impulsively embraced Eva, kissing her on the cheek. "Thank you," she whispered. "Thank you for your confidence in us. We will love her more than you can imagine."

Eva wasn't sure how to respond to the sudden burst of affection, but it made her more confident she'd made the right decision. Janet's little girl would thrive with this tenderhearted, affectionate woman.

When Janet's parents came back to visit her the next morning they found Janet sitting up and looking more like her old self. The color was back in her cheeks and her hair was pulled back neatly from her face. Janet had always complained about what she referred to as her "wild" head of hair. No one could convince her it was one of her most stunning attributes. Her shiny mass of curls looked beautiful regardless of how she wore it.

Janet had decided she would pull herself together and make one final, reasoned attempt to convince her parents she should keep her baby. She inhaled deeply.

"I want to try and make you understand, one more time . . ." Janet began softly, willing herself to keep her emotions in check. "I am seventeen years old and it's not like girls don't have babies all the time at my age, and I think I can be trusted . . ." At the word "trusted" Janet's voice faltered. Her parents had "trusted" her, yet she had proved herself untrustworthy. Because of her, they'd been through more pain and heartache these last few months than they'd experienced in their entire lifetime. They didn't deserve more and she knew she couldn't raise her baby without their help. Janet's eyes filled, in spite of her intentions to remain calm and reasonably make her case, deep down she knew it wouldn't be in the best interests of her baby or her parents.

Her parents stood there, waiting expectantly for her to finish.

"I'll do it," she whispered sadly.

"Oh, sweetheart!" Her mother moved swiftly to her side, holding her close and stroking her hair just as she'd done when Janet was a little girl. "I *knew* you would do the right thing. God will bless you, because *you* are blessing a family with a precious gift they'd lost hope of ever receiving. You'll see, it'll all work out . . ." she pulled back so she could look at Janet's face, the tears streaming down Janet's cheeks. She gently wiped them away and kissed her softly.

"It hurts, Mama. It hurts more than I can describe. I can't imagine it will ever get better."

"But it *will* honey, I promise you . . . it *will* get better. It might take a while but I know God will affirm your selflessness and eventually give you peace that you did the right thing."

Janet's father stood quietly watching his girls, wishing more than anything he could take Janet's pain away. But he couldn't. He leaned in, kissed her on the cheek and whispered how proud they were of her.

How could they possibly be *proud* of her? She'd messed up, messed up in a way she could never have imagined. And yet, here they were, lovingly encouraging her to allow someone else raise the baby she and Brett had created in *one* rash act.

Eva invited Don and Maggie back to the Haven. She wanted to try and explain why she'd decided to give one of Janet's babies to the Davidsons—but away from the clinical coldness of the hospital. She'd begun to feel guilty she hadn't discussed her conundrum with Janet's parents in the first place. She very much wanted them to be in agreement with her. She needed confirmation she was doing the right thing. She didn't want to carry the burden of separating sisters all on her own.

Months ago, when Eva initially shared with Janet and her parents what she knew about the Ryans, they'd been enthusiastic, agreeing they sounded like a perfect match for Janet's baby.

As soon as Maggie and Don sat down, Eva explained her reservations about the Ryans taking both babies, knowing they simply could not afford to take both.

"All these months I've taken comfort in knowing Janet's baby was going to be raised in the Ryan's beautiful little town in upstate New York, yet I don't have peace about their ability to afford both *or* letting them go home with empty arms."

"What options were you considering?" Maggie asked quietly.

Eva shared as much as she knew about the Davidsons, wanting them to understand why she'd considered giving them one of Janet's babies, and that they lived far enough from the Ryans' it was highly unlikely their paths would ever cross.

Maggie was surprisingly agreeable. She readily empathized with how devastated the Ryans would be after making all their preparations.

Maggie had decided early on she wouldn't allow herself to even *see* Janet's baby. Truth be told, Maggie wouldn't even allow herself to get her mind around being a grandmother. It was heartbreaking enough thinking about one grandchild, much less two. She was eager to agree to whatever Eva thought best. Janet wouldn't have any reason to be suspicious about why she was signing two sets of adoption papers.

Maggie was eager to put the whole ordeal behind them, to have Janet home with them and for their lives to return to normal.

Eva breathed a sigh of relief. At least that was settled. She asked how Janet was doing before they left the hospital.

Don and Maggie shared Janet's reluctant, painful acceptance of the need to keep her promise. Eva chided herself for being surprised. She should never have doubted her. Everything she'd grown to know and love about Janet these past months affirmed the incredible strength of character she'd demonstrated today.

"You've raised a remarkable young lady. It's going to be a different place here without her. We're all going to miss her, but I dare say . . ." Eva's voice caught, raw with emotion. "I dare say, no one will miss her more than I."

~ ~

When the three of them arrived back at the hospital and entered Janet's room, they could tell she'd been crying. Her face was blotchy and her eyes were puffy. Someone had provided her with some paper and a pen and she was concentrating on writing. She looked up when they came in, gave a sad smile at their concerned faces.

She was writing her baby girl a prayer, one she hoped she'd be given as soon as she could read. She asked Eva if she thought the Ryans would agree to it. Eva answered she was sure they would. Janet would be meeting them shortly and she could ask them face-to-face.

"There's one more thing. I know it's asking a lot, and they may have already picked out a name . . . but I've been thinking about what I would name her if I could. It's what I've clung to all these months. It's what's gotten me through these last few days. It's what you've all have shown me from the beginning." Janet's throat tightened with emotion. She closed her eyes and willed herself to continue without tears. She drew in a deep breath, opened her eyes and whispered, "*Grace*. Do you think they would agree to name my baby Grace?"

Maggie's eyes filled with tears as she stared at her daughter in wonderment. Despite all that had happened, Janet had clung to her faith. That unquestioning faith. In the end, could Maggie and Don ask for anything greater? Wasn't it the most important thing you could ever wish for your only child—did *anything* else ultimately matter?

Janet shyly handed Eva the prayer she'd so painstakingly written out in her neat cursive handwriting:

> *My sweet baby,*
>
> *I don't know as I write this if you will ever read it, but I pray that someday, when the time is right, your parents will allow you this small glimpse into my heart. I want you to know I loved you so much I put your well being ahead of my own desires. I promise to pray this prayer for you every day as long as I live.*
>
> *"Dear Heavenly Father, please bless this faithful couple You have chosen to be my baby's parents. Direct their lives and give them wisdom to teach her Your truth. Watch and care for this precious child You allowed me to bring into this world. Guide her and direct her. May she acknowledge You early as her Lord and Savior. May she learn to love You with all her heart, soul and strength. May she use the talents You've given her to further Your kingdom. May she realize her body is a temple of the Holy Spirit. Provide for her a husband who loves You above all others and will love her as Christ loves the church. May her life be long and fruitful, filled with the joy and peace that only You can provide. Keep her in the hallow of Your hand until we attain our final goal . . . united forever in the presence of our Lord and Savior, Jesus Christ. Amen."*

Under the prayer she'd written out one of her favorite verses.

> *"For it is by <u>Grace</u> you have been saved through <u>Faith</u>—and this not from yourselves, it is the gift of God." Ephesians 2:8*

Eva read it and passed it over to Maggie and Don. They were all touched, but couldn't help but think about the baby girl Janet knew nothing about. The little girl who wouldn't be given the chance to read her mother's prayer, who wouldn't be named by her.

Eva, thinking quickly, asked Janet if she would write out just what she'd written on another piece of paper.

"It's just that I want to remember your sweet words and pray your prayer with you."

When Janet finished copying her letter, Eva tucked it safely away. Now *both* adoptive parents would have a copy of Janet's prayer.

Later, Eva called the Davidsons back to The Haven, as she wanted to hand deliver Janet's prayer.

Kate's eyes filled as she read Janet's sweet words. Her eyes were drawn to the underlined words in the Bible verse: grace and faith. She knew right then what they would name their little girl: Faith. It would almost be as if Janet had named her, too. Grace and Faith, those great pillars of Christianity.

Faith

1

Eastbrook 1982

Faith tip-toed into the nursery, peeked over the railing of the crib, eyes transfixed on her baby, sleeping peacefully. She watched her sweet mouth suckling in her sleep. What a wonder babies were born knowing how to thrive and mothers were equipped with everything they needed for their babies' growth and sustenance. A sudden surge of love and gratitude made her heart hurt.

She crept out of the room and looked around the house, bed unmade, dishes in the sink—she should use Ella's naptime to do laundry and tidy up. But she wasn't in the mood for housework. She was feeling oddly nostalgic.

She thought of her memory box in the basement. When Faith had moved, she'd haphazardly tossed all of her memorabilia into one big box. Maybe she could use the time to sort through it, create some order out of the chaos.

She hauled the box up from the basement into their bedroom, and dumped all the contents onto the floor.

Where would she even start? She picked up their wedding album.

Had it really been almost four years? Her wedding day had been the happiest day of her life. She remembered it like it was yesterday.

Remembered getting ready to walk down the aisle, not being able to keep herself from sneaking a peek at her handsome groom.

She noticed how his broad shoulders pulled at the seams of his jacket, how his thick, dark hair curled just above his collar. She remembered how serious he'd looked. Goodness! He looked more like a pallbearer than a groom. She'd worried he might not be as excited about getting married as she was, but she needn't have, for as soon as the door opened and the first chords of the bridal march played, his big, familiar grin split his face and stayed there the entire ceremony. His beautiful chocolate brown eyes were filled with such love and desire it made her heart skip.

And then what a glorious night it had been! Their union was the the first time for both of them. That detail had always meant so much to Faith.

He'd been her first love; she'd never even had a serious crush on a guy. She'd worried that she was being too picky. Now she believed God had protected her until the perfect man came along.

After she graduated from high school, she opted not to go to college. After all, all she'd ever wanted to be was a wife and mother. She hadn't been particularly eager to leave the nest either. She'd gotten a job waitressing at a posh restaurant in town. Her parents were disappointed; they worried she'd regret not going to college.

But if it hadn't been for her job waiting tables, she might never have met Matt. She remembered the day he walked in. The attraction had been instant. She begged another waitress to trade tables with her. Matt later told her he'd been smitten the minute she walked up with her dimpled smile and told him about the specials of the day.

Faith had hoped, and half expected, she'd get pregnant on their honeymoon. She'd been ridiculously disappointed when she found out she wasn't.

Month after month the arrival of her period drove her into a temporary depression. Matt knew it was one of "those days" the minute he walked in the door and she didn't greet him with a kiss. Instead, he'd find her lying in bed, tissues clutched in her hands. He'd learned it was best not to try and console her with words, instead he would lay next to her, pull her to him, hold her and silently ask God to give them a baby soon.

Faith worried something was wrong with her. She was young. These were supposed to be the most fertile years of her life. She started researching ways to find out exactly when she was ovulating. She discovered that not only was the *day* important, but even the *time* of day and the *position* of their bodies when they made love. She'd call Matt home from work on those days and hours she deemed most likely to get pregnant.

Matt began to dread those days—there was no spontaneity or tenderness, just cold, clinical mandatory "performances."

Faith convinced him they both needed to be tested. Maybe there was a physiological reason she wasn't conceiving. There wasn't. The doctor had no explanation. His advice was to relax and enjoy the carefree life of newlyweds now, before they were burdened with the responsibility of a child.

It was the wrong thing to say to Faith. How dare he use the term "burden" in conjunction with a baby! She would not be returning to that doctor.

~ ~

For their first anniversary, Matt surprised her with a trip to Florida. They'd be staying at a luxury hotel on a white sandy beach. He knew how much she loved lazing in the sun with a good book.

She was touched by his thoughtfulness. He'd put a lot of effort into making their first anniversary special. He came home with flowers and a beautiful card and had made a reservation at their favorite restaurant.

He was desperate to get her mind off of having a baby and on to enjoying each other the way they did before they got married, before Faith's obsession about getting pregnant. Maybe a week of sunshine, frozen cocktails and sandy beaches would relax her. Maybe anxiety was affecting her ability to conceive.

While his beautiful wife slept in, Matt walked along the shore and prayed, congratulating himself for planning this trip. It was just what they'd *both* needed. Their lovemaking was as tender and passionate as it had been on their honeymoon. There was no insistence on timing or position. They couldn't get enough of each other. He prayed their enlivened lovemaking created the new life Faith so desperately wanted.

A week after returning from their glorious vacation, Faith started her period. It rendered the worst bout of depression yet. They'd prayed so hard! *Why* was God withholding a gift they desired so much?

Matt's heart sunk when he pulled into the driveway and saw the shades lowered on all the windows.

He entered their darkened bedroom and sat on the side of the bed. When he pulled her up against him, she pressed her face against his warm chest, listening to the steady thud of his heartbeat.

"Oh, honey. I'm sorry. But trust me," he gently lifted her chin to look at him, "I know it's going to happen. In *His* perfect timing."

"Why? Why is He making us wait?"

"Sweetheart. You're twenty years old! I'm sure you could safely have babies for the next twenty years. Please, *please* let's just enjoy each other. I *need* my old Faith back, I *need* to know I'm more to you than just a stud horse." He was only half joking.

Faith couldn't help but give him her dimpled smile. Matt gently kissed the tears on her cheeks, before placing his mouth over hers.

A few months after their vacation, she decided maybe their problem was they made love too much. They would take a month off. She didn't even allow him to kiss her that month. She thought it would be too hard to stop at just kissing, and she was determined to carry out this experiment. It wasn't a good month for Matt.

On their second anniversary, Faith's expectations were high. Perhaps he would surprise her with another beach vacation? Maybe somewhere more exotic?

When Matt came in from work, she'd greeted him more passionately than usual. He'd responded just as she knew he would.

Afterwards, they lingered in bed and Faith snuggled up to his warm body, resting her head on his broad chest. "I'm so happy you're mine," she sighed.

Matt didn't respond and Faith lifted her head to look at him. He wasn't smiling and his big brown eyes looked at her sadly. "Are you *really* happy, Faith? Do you think you could be happy with just me?"

She didn't answer right away. She didn't even want to contemplate a life without children. Unconvincingly, she finally answered, "Of course I could. It's just not what I envisioned."

She jumped up, not liking the turn of their conversation. "Let me go grab your gift."

She came back in, eager for him to read his card and open his gift. She'd gotten him a bottle of his favorite cologne and a blue golf shirt she knew he'd look great in. She'd written something witty, something she was sure he'd appreciate.

"Aw. That's great, honey. Thank you." He didn't laugh like she'd hoped he would. He didn't kiss her or pull her into his arms like he normally would. Instead, he reached over to the nightstand and grabbed his card. "Sorry, I didn't get a chance to shop for a gift."

She secretly grinned, thinking the surprise tickets must be enclosed. It was a beautiful card, but he'd only written five words, "Happy Anniversary, I love you."

Was this a joke? Usually he wrote all sorts of flowery stuff, listing all the reasons he loved her, how thankful he was God had given him a beautiful wife, perfect for him in every way. She loved his cards. She felt a stab of disappointment. Had he really not gotten her a gift?

"Thank you." She forced a smile and leaned in to give him a kiss. Matt held her back from him, his eyes unreadable.

She felt a small frisson of fear at this unsmiling, serious Matt.

He gave a deep sigh, swung his legs over the side of the bed and stood up. He picked his pants up off the floor and slowly pulled them on before turning back to her. With his back against the wall, he folded his arms against his bare chest. "It hasn't been a good year, Faith. I couldn't bring myself to carry on like it has, or write things that made it seem like it was all hunky-dory between us."

Faith felt her heart constricting. *What was he talking about? How could he think things weren't "hunky-dory?"*

"What do you mean?" she asked in an almost whisper. She couldn't stand him thinking their marriage was less than perfect, that he was finding *her* less than perfect.

"Think about it, Faith. All you've cared about since the day we got home from our honeymoon is getting pregnant. I've tried to be patient. I've begged for a baby just as earnestly as you have. But, unlike you, I know I'd be happy even if we never could have a baby. I'm a distant second to your desire to have a baby. I don't want to be a distant second."

"You're not second Matt. You can't believe that." Faith's voice was strained, tears filled her eyes.

Had she given him a reason to believe things weren't good between them? She thought back through the last few years. It *had* been all about her. She never considered what a toll her disappointment and frustration took on him. She thought about the month she wouldn't even let him kiss her. She thought of the week after they'd returned from Florida, how she'd never even gotten out of bed. Matt's attempts to comfort her had been met with coldness.

Please Lord, let me make it up to him. Forgive me for not putting him first.

She walked over to him, looped her arms around his neck, pressed her lips into the hallow of his neck. "Please forgive me. It never occurred to me how selfish I've been. How I've made you feel. Please, I couldn't bear it if you stopped loving me."

"I didn't say I stopped loving you. I just said things weren't good."

"Well, I can't bear you thinking things aren't 'good' either. I want you to think things are fantastic. I'm going to change. I'm going to concentrate on us . . . on *you*. Things will be different from now on, I promise. You *are* enough for me, and I'll prove it to you. I really will."

She got on her tiptoes, placing her lips on his. He finally uncrossed him arms, and held her close. "I sure hope so, Faith."

Matt sounded doubtful. He would believe it when he saw it.

But Faith made good on her promise. He knew it wasn't easy for her. He knew each month she didn't get pregnant brought her deep sadness. But instead of becoming hardened in the midst of her pain, she came to him and took comfort in his arms and in his prayers.

The thought of Matt not being happy with her had hurt, but it had scared her too. She felt like she'd go crazy if he stopped loving her. God had given her the man of her dreams. How awful she hadn't been the wife he deserved.

Ten months after their second anniversary, Faith missed her period. She wouldn't allow herself to get too excited, but after three days she ran out and got a pregnancy test. She cried tears of joy when the telling blue line appeared so quickly.

When she heard Matt's car pull in the driveway after work, she jumped up and met him at the door with the test.

"Does this mean what I think it means?"

"Oh, Matt," she said softly, her eyes brimming with tears. "We are going to have a baby!"

"Yes!" He whooped. He picked her up and swung her around, held her tight and silently thanked God for answering their prayers.

And now their little Ella was three months old. Faith wondered if God, in His infinite wisdom, had withheld the precious gift of their baby until she learned to put Matt first.

She continued to look through their wedding pictures. She lovingly traced her finger along Matt's dear grin. She was still crazy in love with him. In him, God had given her immeasurably more than she could have asked for or imagined, just like the Bible promised.

She set the wedding album aside and her eyes were drawn to the tattered piece of paper her birth mother had written a prayer on. Faith remembered how devastated she'd been to learn she wasn't her parents "real" daughter. She was deeply hurt that her real mother hadn't wanted her. She told her mom she had absolutely no desire to ever meet her. And yet, for some reason she'd kept this prayer all these years.

It was only since she'd had Ella that Faith began thinking about her birth mother. Wondering what she looked like, where she lived. Wondered if she had any other siblings.

She couldn't imagine *any* set of circumstances that would have allowed her to give Ella up. But things were different back then. Women having children out of wedlock were shamed and scorned. Both she and her young mother would have lived with a stigma. She felt a grudging sympathy for her that she'd never felt before. Reading the words of the prayer ". . . *May she learn to love you with all her heart, soul and strength . . . Provide for her a husband who loves You above all others and will love her as Christ loves the church . . .*" brought tears to her eyes. Every request had been answered. Perhaps it *was* an act of selflessness and love to give her to a couple that might give her a better life, and Faith *had* lived a charmed life. She couldn't imagine a life without her parents and her adopted brothers, couldn't imagine loving another woman the way she loved the only mom she'd ever known. They *were* her "real" family, in the end it hadn't mattered a whit whom had given birth to her.

For the first time, Faith wanted to meet her birth mother. She wanted to tell her in person that she'd done the right thing, the selfless thing.

She'd been so engrossed in looking at pictures and thinking about her birth mother that the time had gotten away from her and before she knew it, Ella was awake from her nap. Faith left all the contents of the box strewn on the floor.

Sunshine poured into the nursery. It was finally nice enough outside to take Ella out.

"Ready to get outside in the sunshine and go see Gramma, Ella-Bella?" Faith nuzzled the soft skin under Ella's chin. Oh, that sweet smell! If only it could be bottled.

No one could deny Ella was a beautiful baby. Faith had hoped their baby would have Matt's eyes. At first they'd been an unidentifiable color, but now they were the most beautiful shade of green. Her eyes tilted up at the corners—unlike her's or Matt's. Faith wondered if her eyes came from her real mother or father. Yet another reason she wanted to find them, to know who they were and what they looked like.

After she nursed Ella, she lovingly dressed her and put her in her car seat. After carefully strapping her into the back seat, they set out.

She decided to take the scenic route, avoid the city traffic. She drove along and marveled at the bright sunshine, the new buds on the trees, the daffodils in bloom.

"Isn't it beautiful, Ella-Bella? Can you see the pretty flowers and the blue sky?"

Ella cooed contently. Faith tilted her rearview mirror to look at her. Admired her chubby, flushed cheeks, her big eyes and long eyelashes. Staring into the rearview mirror, she never knew she drifted across the lane into an oncoming truck.

2

They said Faith died instantly.

The driver's side was completely crushed. The impact had spun the car off the road but it had miraculously come to rest on the soft new grass just shy of the trunk of a large tree, leaving the passenger side untouched.

The paramedics knew instantly Faith hadn't survived by the angle of her head, her beautiful face too bloodied to recognize. The infant in the backseat appeared untouched, looking to all the world like any normal baby, crying piteously, but not hysterically.

It didn't seem right for the birds to still be singing or the sun to be reflecting so brightly off the mangled metal. Not in the midst of such devastation.

When the ambulance arrived, they couldn't open the passenger door because of the tree. They had to wait for the Jaws of Life to pry the crushed metal away from the driver's side and then climb carefully into the back seat and unbuckle the infant.

One of the paramedics passed the infant into the waiting arms of his co-worker, who clasped her tightly to him. She quieted immediately, laying her head on his shoulder. Tears filled his eyes. Life wasn't fair. He would never get used to arriving on to horrific scenes like this, young lives snuffed out way before their time.

~ ~

Matt pulled into the driveway of their small house. Faith had fallen in love with it at first sight, especially the big porch. Matt hadn't seen the potential. He tried to talk her into something newer. She'd said the newer houses didn't hold near the charm.

Matt couldn't resist giving into her enthusiastic vision. He remembered her excitement the day they'd closed on it. True to her vision, she'd turned it into a charming, cozy home.

Matt sighed contentedly, there was nothing like coming home after a long day and being greeted by his beautiful wife.

He was disappointed when he noticed Faith's car wasn't in the driveway. He knew she'd taken Ella out to see her mom, but normally she would have called if she hadn't planned on being home before him.

He loosened his tie as he walked into the kitchen, removed his sport coat, hung it over the back of a chair. He noticed with surprise what a mess she'd left. Faith always tidied up before he came home. The first signs of alarm coursed through him. It looked like she'd left in a hurry. Had something happened that she'd had to rush off?

He walked into their bedroom. The bed was unmade. Her memory box was upended, its contents scattered all over the floor.

He picked up the receiver from the phone on the nightstand. He began dialing his in-laws but the doorbell rang before he finished. He put the phone back in its cradle and went to answer the door.

His heart leapt in his chest when he opened it to a somber policeman.

"Are you Matthew Connors?"

"Yes. Why?" Matt whispered hoarsely.

"There's been an accident involving your wife and baby." The officer explained briefly what happened. "I'm sorry to say your wife didn't survive but your baby, miraculously, appears to be in good condition. They were both taken to Memorial Hospital."

Matt was too stunned to speak. He stared at the policeman, willing this to be a bad dream.

"I could drive you to the hospital," the officer offered.

"No. No thanks. I . . . uh . . . I can drive myself." He closed the door without saying another word, not wanting to look at the pitying face of the police officer another minute.

Matt pressed his forehead against the closed door. This could *not* be happening. There must be some kind of mix up. Faith was a cautious driver, especially with Ella in the car. He would go up to the hospital and they would clear it up; it would all work out. Surely it was a mistake.

He walked back into the bedroom to grab his wallet and keys. What a mess! Suddenly the sight of it filled him with fury. He roughly gathered up every album, card, and picture and shoved them back into the box. He carried it down to the basement, dropped it on the floor, and angrily kicked it into a corner.

Why had Faith been in such a hurry? It wasn't like her. How could she have been so reckless? The truck driver had told the policeman that when she drifted over into his lane, he hadn't had time to react.

Matt went through the motions at the hospital like an automaton, flatly answering questions, filling out paperwork, stiffly hugging people, thanking them for coming. He numbly watched Faith's devastated parents and brothers try to grapple with the reality that they'd never (in this life anyway) see their precious daughter and sister again.

It was only when he began filling out Ella's discharge papers that he realized he was expected to take Ella with him. He couldn't take her home! He didn't know the first thing about taking care of her. He'd rarely bathed her, he hadn't even changed many diapers.

The hospital staff was sympathetic. They treated him like a brand new father, sent him home with bottles of formula, walked him through every step of her care.

He resignedly carried Ella out in her car seat and carefully buckled her in. She slept through the ride home but began to cry as soon as he pulled into the driveway. He carried her in, getting her out of her car seat as quickly as he could. Ella's crying turned into screaming, her little face becoming beet red.

He laid her in her crib while he fixed a bottle. He warmed the formula like the nurses had shown him and sat down to feed her. She quieted momentarily, recognizing she was going to be fed, but as soon as the nipple touched her mouth she stiffened and started screaming again. She didn't want any part of the bottle, she'd only been nursed. Matt tried everything to get her to take it. Her voice was getting hoarse from screaming. She would *not* take it. She only wanted Faith.

For more than an hour Matt tried everything he knew to comfort her, to stop the screaming and stiffening. He felt like shaking her in frustration. How could such a thought enter his head? It horrified him, scared him so much he decided to lay her back in her crib. Tears of sadness, frustration and inadequacy filled his eyes as he walked into the kitchen to call his mother-in-law, Kate.

Even though it was past midnight, she agreed to come. Unbelievably enough, Ella was *still* crying when she got there. How many hours could a baby cry before passing out?

Kate picked Ella up, held her close, tears filling her own eyes. She finally quieted Ella down and got her to drink her bottle. Dawn was breaking by the time Kate gently laid the sleeping, spent Ella back in her crib. She assured Matt she was only a phone call away should she need him.

Matt fell into an exhausted sleep. Ella's crying awakened him. *Why wasn't Faith getting her?* Usually, she got to her so fast he never even heard Ella crying. It had made Faith laugh when he'd said he couldn't believe Ella had slept through the night their very first night home from the hospital. He reached over to nudge her—felt the emptiness.

The awful reality hit him. Faith's warm body would never lie next to his again. He would never kiss her warm, Faith-scented skin. Never hear her sweet voice. Never see her beloved dimpled smile. The weight of his sadness took his breath away.

The awful, fearful anxiety returned with the realization that the angry little baby in the next room was his responsibility alone.

Matt thought he was going to go crazy in the house. The quietness and the evidence of Faith everywhere he looked left his heart constricted every minute. He began to spend as much of his days as he could at his in-laws.

He knew he was relying on Kate too much, but he didn't know what else to do. Kate didn't have the heart to refuse to help care for Ella and it filled some of the void in her heart that Faith had left. The attention Ella required was the only solace she had.

Matt surprised everyone when he decided to return to work just a week after the funeral. He needed to be *doing* something. He needed the distraction from the reality of losing Faith.

Kate agreed to keep Ella for him. For the sake of convenience, more and more of Ella's baby gear was transferred to the Davidson household. She began spending every weekday night there. It made it easier. It didn't make sense for Matt to wake her up each morning just to take her to her grandparents.

3

Eastbrook 1984

Life had fallen into a predictable pattern. The family had plodded through the days, months and eventually years without Faith. Ella was a thankful distraction for everyone. Matt worked more and more hours but spent his weekends with Ella, trying to be both mother and father to her.

Ella would be three years old in February, and she was still spending the bulk of her time at her grandparents. Matt was someone she played with after dinner and stayed with on the weekends.

Kate knew Matt thought he was doing what was best for Ella, but she knew it wasn't what Faith would have wanted. As much as Kate would love to raise Ella as her own, she knew it wouldn't be fair to Matt or Ella. They needed to bond as father and daughter.

John and Kate agreed to have the discussion with Matt together. They'd both felt convicted Matt needed to take full responsibility for raising his and Faith's only child. Ella needed to be back in her own bed, she needed to *live* in her home, not just visit it on the weekends.

Matt worried how Ella would respond to the quietness of their little home compared to the constant activity at the Davidson's.

They needn't do it cold turkey, Kate assured him. She would continue to watch Ella a few days a week at Matt's and a few days at their house. But it was time for Kate to concentrate on being the full-time mother to Faith's brothers, time for Matt to find and hire a full-time nanny enabling Ella to grow up in her own home.

Once Matt got used to taking care of Ella, he loved coming home to her. His nights were still lonely, but they were less lonely. All because Kate and John had seen what he hadn't. He and Ella needed each other, he needed this bond with his only child. She provided him more fulfillment and joy than he could have dreamed possible.

He prayed expectantly for God to provide the perfect person to care for her while he was at work. She was his little girl and together they would become the family he knew Faith would have wanted them to be.

Grace

1

October 1975

The air was crisp and cool. Bright lights lit up the football field. The bleachers were full of parents and students eager to watch the game.

Grace had taken extra time with her hair and make-up. The humidity was low, so there was a good chance her hair would stay flat and smooth, feathered back with a curling iron roll on each side of her face. After the game she and her friends, Deb and Cathy, were going to their first high school party.

Grace thought Deb and Cathy were acting a little weird. At halftime, they pulled Grace behind the bleachers and pulled out a little plastic bag.

"What's that?" Grace asked, even though she knew what it was.

"A bag of fun," Deb joked. Cathy giggled like it was the funniest thing she'd ever heard.

Deb carefully rolled a joint. Obviously, it wasn't the first time. She lit it, took a long toke and passed it to Grace.

"Come on, Grace. It might be just what you need to loosen up a little."

"You know I won't." She folded her arms against her chest, close to tears. Drugs scared her and she knew if her parents ever found out she'd even *thought* about smoking pot they'd be devastated. She was their world; she could never hurt them like that.

Cathy and Deb continued passing the joint back and forth.

She felt betrayed that her friends had hid this from her. They knew her well enough to know she wouldn't have gone for it, that's why they never told her about it. Where did they even get the stuff?

When Cathy and Deb finally finished the joint, Deb turned to her, "Come on, Grace. Don't be such a goody-two-shoes. Dale's supposed to be at the party. Maybe a few tokes would give you the confidence to talk to him."

"Dale wouldn't be interested in a burnout."

"Because he's such a good church boy?" Deb asked.

Cathy rolled her eyes, "Yeah, sure he is."

"For your information, he *is*."

Deb and Cathy exchanged knowing looks.

Grace was torn. It hurt that Deb and Cathy had kept this from her. The three of them had been friends since elementary school and now she suddenly felt like an unwelcome third wheel. But she really wanted to see Dale and she didn't have anyone else to go to the party with.

Dale was her current "crush." He was the only guy from her church who went to her school, too.

A few weeks ago, the youth group had gone to a youth rally. The only reason Grace wanted to go was the possibility that Dale might make a rare appearance.

Just as the bus was ready to pull out, she spotted his cool car pulling into the parking lot. Her heart started racing.

He'd boarded the bus with his confident swagger. Scoping out whom he might grace with his presence. His eyes met Grace's, and he strode purposely to her seat.

"Any one sitting here?"

She blushed, "Just me."

He'd slid in next to her, deliberately pressing his knee against hers as they talked.

He sat next to her at the rally, too. She felt the jealous looks of the other girls. He leaned in so close to ask her questions, she could feel his warm breath on her neck. She found herself staring at his mouth when he talked. She wondered what it would feel like to have his lips on hers.

Back on the bus, he asked for her phone number and offered her a ride home. Grace's heart sank when the bus pulled into the church parking lot and she saw her parents already there waiting for her. *Shucks.* But he took her phone number—surely that meant he was planning on asking her out?

But when she ran into him in the hall at school the following Monday, surrounded by all of his popular friends, he barely acknowledged her.

She *would* go to the party, it would be worth putting up with Cathy and Deb to be singled out by him. She could just picture all the jealous looks she'd get when he only had eyes for her, just like the girls from church.

As they approached the house hosting the party, Grace's heart beat faster. She was nervous about hanging out with Dale and his popular friends. She'd always been painfully shy, but she reminded herself how he'd acted at the rally, how he'd asked for her phone number. Surely he'd be happy to see her.

The house was dark and there were groups of kids outside smoking. The yard was so crowded that they had to squeeze their way through groups to get into the house.

Grace's eyes scanned the room looking for Dale. He was tall and would be easy to spot. Sure enough, she glimpsed him as he and some friends slipped out the sliding door to the patio. She took a deep breath, willed her heart to stop racing and made her way over to his group.

He was laughing with friends and didn't see her approach. She tapped his shoulder, "Hey Dale. I thought you might be here."

He turned around and looked at her and for a few awful seconds she thought he was going to act like he didn't even know who she was.

"'Hey' yourself," he finally answered. He didn't appear particularly happy to see her.

"I haven't seen you at church since the rally . . ."

"Nope," he cut her off. "Church isn't exactly my favorite place to be . . ." He laughed and his friends laughed with him.

*What? Was he embarrassed to talk about his faith with his school friends? Embarrassed to even admit he **goes** to church?*

Grace looked at him closer. His eyes were bloodshot and he seemed a little unsteady.

"Where have you been hiding your pretty little church girl, Dale?" One of his friends looked Grace up and down. "Mmmm, I like what I see."

Grace felt her face flame with color. She felt like a fool. "Uh . . . I'm gonna go find my friends." She turned and glared at Dale. "See ya round, Dale." She started to walk away, but Dale grasped her elbow and led her to a more private place in the backyard.

"I was shocked to see you here. I didn't think you went to parties like this." Dale was slurring his words and Grace could smell the pot and alcohol on his breath. She was as shocked and hurt to see him like this as she'd been with Deb and Cathy earlier.

"I only came because I thought you might be here, that we might talk. I thought you'd be different." Grace couldn't believe she admitted he was the only reason she came. As if he needed more to puff up his already big head.

He ignored her, went back to what she'd said initially. "You said you wanted to meet up and talk? Are you sure you just wanted to talk?" He took her hand and led her out to the garage. He turned her around and backed her against the wall, placed his hands against the wall above her shoulders. "You had more in mind than just talking. Come on, admit it. You wanted to hook up with me."

He leaned down, clamped his lips on her neck, grabbed her and pulled her into him.

Grace ducked under his arm and walked away, disgusted. *Yuck.* She was furious and felt violated. What a loser. A fake. A phony. What had she been thinking? She should have known when he barely acknowledged her in the halls he was a two-faced hypocrite.

She had to sneak around the darkened house to find a phone to call her parents. She asked them to come get her, told them she'd be on the corner waiting. She slipped out without saying another word to anyone. Lesson learned. No more high school parties for her.

2

The following week at Wednesday night's youth group Dale acted like he hadn't seen her at the party. Had he been too high and drunk to remember?

The youth pastor asked Dale to start their meeting with a word of prayer. Dale broke into his usual sincere sounding prayer, "Father God, may our eyes and ears be open to hearing from You, may hearts be changed . . ." *yada, yada*. It sickened her to listen to him. When she couldn't stomach it any longer, she loudly pushed back her chair mid-prayer and walked out of the room.

How could someone be that fake? Were all the kids in youth group one person at church and another around their school friends? She might never know. What she *did* know was she wasn't going to spend another Wednesday night watching that idiot be fawned over for what he clearly wasn't.

Grace's parents said skipping Wednesday night church wasn't an option. If she refused to attend youth group she would have to join them. Grace had to weigh up which would be more dreadful. Her parent's Wednesday nights were spent "calling." She found the practice mortifying.

"Calling" consisted of meeting at the church and dividing into small groups. After a few minutes of praying for bold words and softened hearts, and loaded down with tracts, they'd set out traipsing through neighborhoods "calling" on people. Grace found it hard to believe they'd get any converts. She thought they were more likely to turn people *off* of Jesus rather than *on* to Him.

On her first Wednesday night of calling, Grace was linked up with three middle-aged couples. They were sincere; they did what they did because they had a genuine desire to share what they knew to be true: the only way to Heaven was to have a personal relationship with Jesus. They didn't want anyone to be left behind when Christ returned.

On this particular night, they chose to canvas a well-to-do neighborhood near the church. Grace lagged behind the rest of the group, doing her best to remain invisible. House after house they were greeted with thinly veiled impatience. Most would at least grudgingly agree to take a tract.

Grace was surprised the group didn't get discouraged. Snub after snub, they pressed on.

Grace was enjoying peeking into the doors and windows of the warmly lit homes. She'd never seen such big, beautiful houses and tried to imagine what it would be like to live in one of them.

Trudging up to one of the last houses in the neighborhood, they were surprisingly greeted like expected guests.

"Come in out of the chill! I'll brew a pot of coffee."

Grace didn't have any choice but to shuffle reluctantly into the home with the adults. She was amazed this family actually seemed grateful someone cared enough about their eternal destiny to trudge around their neighborhood with tracts. When they saw Grace they called up to their daughter to come down and meet her.

A beautiful girl came skipping down the stairs. *How lucky to be rich* ***and*** *perfect looking.*

The girl had long, dark shiny hair, beautiful skin and an enviably cute shape. Grace blushed with embarrassment at being thrust upon her.

"Hi! I'm Annie. You wanna come up and see my room?" She smiled warmly at Grace, acting eager to make a new friend.

"I'm Grace." She returned Annie's smile gratefully, following her up the spiral staircase. *Phew, at least she wouldn't have to sit and listen to the tedious Roman's Road to Salvation.*

"You must not go to my school, because I know I'd remember you," Annie said over her shoulder as she cleared a space on her bed and indicated Grace take a seat.

"No, I go to Western High—we just go to church here."

"I'm supposed to be up here cleaning my room. Ugh." Annie sighed as she turned a shirt inside right and hung it up in her closet. "It's going to take forever to put away all these clothes."

Grace had never seen so many clothes. There must have been a dozen outfits lying on the floor.

"You *do* have a lot of clothes."

"Too many. I guess I like shopping too much." She looked back over at Grace. "I love your hair! I wish I had curls like that." She chattered away like they'd been friends forever.

"You wouldn't like it if you had it. I wish I had *your* hair."

"I guess we always want what we don't have." Annie smiled. "So you came over to talk to us about Jesus?"

Sadly, Grace was mortified, it sounded so pushy and judgmental. She should be ashamed of herself! She should *want* to do everything she could that all might be saved. She believed with all her heart that Jesus *was* "the Way, the Truth and the Life." How could she possibly feel uncomfortable sharing that?

"Kind of." Grace reluctantly admitted. *Kind of?*

Annie sensed her discomfort and wanted to put her at ease ". . . or did you just want to invite us to your church?"

"Yes." *Why did that sound so much more acceptable?*

Annie didn't miss a beat. "I went to my friend's church once. Went on a hayride. Does your church do fun things like that?"

"Sometimes. It's just that . . . I don't know, there aren't really any fun people in my youth group."

"Do you have a boyfriend?"

Grace couldn't help but smile at her endless stream of questions. Easily jumping from one subject to another.

"No. Do you?"

"No. There's this one guy I have a crush on, but he's going with someone."

"Yeah, I had a crush on a guy too. But he ended up being a jerk. He's the real reason I don't want to go to youth group."

"How was he a jerk?"

Surprisingly, Grace told her the whole story. What a phony he was. "He's Mister Popular at school and at church, but two completely different people . . . it's sickening."

"He sounds like a jerk. So I guess that means you don't smoke pot."

"No. Never. Do you?"

Annie lowered her voice. "Sometimes. Don't want the 'parental units' to hear me." She winked conspiratorially.

Grace loved her honesty, couldn't help but smile at her candor. "What do you like about it?"

"I don't know. I guess I do it because all my friends do it and it seems like the cool thing to do." She shook out a pair of jeans. "We're about the same size . . . you want to borrow these?'

Grace hardly knew how to respond to such friendliness and generosity from a virtual stranger.

She would **love** to borrow them—but when would she see her to give them back?

"Oh, that's okay. But thanks. That's really nice of you."

"It's not like I don't have gobs of clothes."

To Grace's disappointment, too soon Annie's mom called up and said the group was getting ready to leave.

Annie tore a sheet of paper out of a spiral notebook, jotted down her number and gave it to Grace. "Call me and we can go hang out at the mall sometime."

Grace tucked the piece of paper in the front pocket of her jeans, hoping they really *would* get together.

The group of callers were buoyant about their visit. They said having all those doors slammed in their faces was all worth it, just to be able to touch *one* family with their message. "Obviously, Jesus paved the way and the Spirit softened their hearts."

One of the women turned to look back at Grace, "And look at *you,* Grace! Here it was your very first night of calling and you were able to witness to another teenager."

Grace didn't want to admit that it was Annie who had reached out to *her,* that she'd been a complete failure at "witnessing."

3

The following Sunday, Annie and her parents came to their church. The "calling" group was thrilled and secretly, so was Grace.

When they met up in the narthex after the service, she and Annie picked up right where they'd left off the night they met. There weren't any awkward silences, and Annie didn't even do all the talking. Grace felt free to be herself. She made Annie laugh almost as much as Annie made *her* laugh.

Annie wanted to go to youth group. "Who cares if most of them are phonies? We're not. Plus, they do fun stuff."

Grace finally gave in, most of the events included more than just their church's small youth group anyway. It was a chance to meet more boys. They'd make their own fun. And the best part? No more "calling."

Grace started to enjoy youth group, Annie made it fun. They were often called out for laughing too much. Everyone was drawn to Annie. Even Dale The Jerk tried to work his charm on her. Predictably, Annie didn't give him the time of day, and he finally got the hint and stopped trying.

But Annie didn't go just for the fun. She hadn't been brought up believing in God. She had never prayed or knew anything about the Bible.

It was all new and exciting to her. She loved the Bible lessons, loved sharing what the verses meant to her. She got choked up at every rally.

Her enthusiasm touched Grace. She was almost envious that Annie felt things so deeply. It made her wonder about the depth of her own faith. Some of the speakers at the rallies could bring even the most hardened teenagers to tears, yet her eyes remained as dry as dust. Was her faith in Jesus about nothing more than a free ticket to Heaven? Did she not love Him enough to shed a few tears for His ultimate sacrifice?

She'd taken her faith for granted. Yet, *surely* she was saved. She distinctly remembered praying with her mom at her bedside and asking Jesus into her heart. But she remembered feeling relief more than anything else. She had been terrified her parents would go to Heaven without her.

Annie's faith wasn't based on relief or fear, hers was based on humble gratitude and love. She was able to see God's hand in everything that happened to her.

"Just think," she told Grace, "if it hadn't been for Dale The Jerk, I wouldn't have met you! God planned for us to be best friends."

Grace never considered that, but it was true—she would ***never*** have agreed to go "calling" if it had not been for Dale being such a phony. *Thank you, Lord, for giving me Annie just when I needed her most and please help me* ***feel*** *the way she does. Please let my faith not just be in my head, but in my heart, too.*

4

Annie knew from the time she was a little girl where she was going to college—the same one her parents had graduated from. Her family still took road trips down to watch the big football games. Grace went with them once. She could see why Annie loved it. The campus was beautiful; it was everything one dreamed a university campus would look like.

As they entered their senior year of high school, Grace dreaded Annie leaving her. She would miss her terribly. But, the ever-hopeful Annie refused to give up on the idea that Grace would go with her. Grace wouldn't let herself believe it; she knew her parents couldn't afford to send her there.

"We'll figure something out," Annie vowed. "Maybe you could get a scholarship."

Grace *was* an excellent student. She'd always gotten straight A's and scored way above average on the SAT.

Mrs. Erickson, Grace's ninth grade English teacher, was the reason Grace strived so hard to excel. She had convinced Grace she was a gifted writer.

The end of Grace's junior year, Mrs. Erickson helped her apply for all kinds of scholarships and grants. She thought it might be possible that Grace's parents' small income might qualify her for some Federal grant money, too.

Annie remained confident God would answer their prayers and pave a way for them to go together.

Grace would never forget the day she got the acceptance letter and offer of a full ride scholarship. She couldn't wait to show it to Annie, who predictably squealed with excitement and pulled her into a bear hug. They jumped up and down like little kids. When she stepped back there were tears in Annie's eyes, "I just *knew* God was going to make this happen!"

They spent most of the summer planning how they would decorate their dorm room.

They loved college life just as much as they'd envisioned. They became close friends with a few of the girls on their hall. They got involved with Campus Crusade. They pulled crazy pranks and went to plenty of parties.

Grace loved her classes, particularly her English classes. One of her professors convinced her to pursue journalism.

Annie decided she wanted to be a teacher. Grace knew she'd make a wonderful teacher—she was great with kids. She even volunteered to teach Sunday school at the church they attended.

Yes, college life was everything Grace hoped it would be. It was perfect until Jimmy Jackson transferred there their junior year.

Grace would never forget the first time Annie saw him. He strolled into church late, not at all self-conscious, walking conspicuously down the center aisle looking for somewhere to sit. Grace felt Annie sit up straighter in the pew, straining to get a better look at him. He found a seat two pews in front of them and must have felt Annie's eyes on him, because he looked around and met her gaze and it was like they were the only two people in the church.

After the benediction, Jimmy managed to finagle himself around the parishioners until he was walking out with them.

He introduced himself, asking if they were students at the university. After he shared he'd just transferred in, Annie asked him if he'd like to walk to the cafeteria with them. Of course, he jumped at the opportunity. They tried to include Grace in their easy conversation, but she felt like an outsider anyway. She made an excuse to leave as soon as she finished eating.

Annie told her later that they'd lingered and talked so much they'd had to be thrown out of the cafeteria. Then when he walked her to their dorm he asked if he could take her out Friday night. Annie was tickled pink.

Annie came in from that first date and announced Jimmie was going to be the man she married and Grace didn't doubt it. He started going to church with them every Sunday, even volunteered with Annie to teach Sunday school. No doubt about it, they had it bad for each other and Grace knew she'd never have Annie all to herself ever again.

It wasn't like Annie completely deserted her—she always made sure she reserved a night just for the two of them. Even joining her at a few parties that didn't include Jimmy. But it was never the same, and Grace couldn't help but wish she would find her own "Jimmy."

5

All week Annie had been anticipating her date with Jimmy. He'd asked her to dress up because he was taking her somewhere special. When he came to pick her up he whistled appreciatively.

"Wow! You look beautiful!" Every time he looked at Annie, he marveled at her beauty. But she wasn't just beautiful on the outside, she was beautiful on the inside too. Jimmy had never met anyone with a sweeter spirit.

He took her to an expensive restaurant on the river. When they arrived they were led to the best seat in the house, with a beautiful view of the water. The tables were candle lit. A band played soft music in front of a small dance floor. Jimmy pulled out her chair for her, before sitting down himself. He reached over the table for her hands. He pulled one of them up to his lips and kissed her knuckles tenderly, never taking his eyes off of her.

"Do you have any idea how much I love you? How much I thank God for you?" He spoke softly, seriously.

"You know I feel the same way."

"Let's order an appetizer and then dance."

After they'd given their order, he grasped her hand and led her out to the dance floor.

He nodded to the band, and they started playing one of their favorites, Champaign's "How 'bout Us."

It touched her that he'd arranged every detail.

He pulled her against him and Annie marveled at how perfectly their bodies melded together.

She nestled her head contentedly on his shoulder as they slowly danced, listening to the familiar words of the song.

When the song ended and they returned to their seats a bottle of champagne sat chilling on the table. *Wow. He really had pulled out all the stops.*

Jimmy poured them each a glass, then raised his, signaling for a toast. As his glass touched her's he said, "'How '***bout*** us?" He echoed the words of the song, "'Some people are made for each other . . . last through all kinds of weather . . .'"

Annie's brown eyes danced as their glasses clinked together. Was this a marriage proposal? He didn't produce a ring, still, she had hoped this was what this special night was all about.

Their graduation was just around the corner, after that they wouldn't be seeing each other every day.

Dinner was delicious. As usual, Jimmy kept her laughing. He talked excitedly about the job he'd been offered. She was excited for him, too. She was especially excited it wasn't too far from where her parents lived. She had to bite back asking him if she should start applying for teaching jobs in the same city. She didn't want it to be *her* idea, didn't want to *assume* anything. In all his talk, he never said "we." Maybe she was wrong in believing he didn't want to move on to the next chapter of his life without her. Maybe he wasn't ready to "pop the question" after all.

Annie figured Jimmy provided the band with a playlist—every song they played was a familiar one. She didn't want the night to end.

As they left the restaurant, he suggested a walk down by the river. He guided her over to a bench and then gently forced her to sit.

He knelt before her, taking her hands in his, softly kissing the tops of them.

This is it, Annie thought. He's going to ask me to marry him. Instead he stood back up, stretched out his back, loosened his tie. He sighed deeply before finally sitting down next to her, resting his arm casually along the bench behind her. He looked out at the river. Annie followed his gaze. He pulled her closer against him, gently tipped her chin up to meet his gaze.

"Have you had a good night, Annie?"

"The best," she whispered.

"Is there anything that could make it better?"

There is one thing that could make it better, she thought, but didn't answer. He lowered his lips to hers, kissing her long and deep.

"I love you, Annie. I want to spend the rest of my life with you, have babies with you and grow old with you . . ." He dropped down on one knee in front of her. "Will you marry me?"

"Oh, Jimmy." Tears filled Annie's eyes.

"Is that a yes?"

"Yes! Yes! Yes! From our first date, I couldn't picture my life without you in it."

Jimmy reached into his pocket, brought out a ring and slipped it on her finger. It was beautiful.

"It's the prettiest ring I've ever seen! Did someone help you pick it out? Was Grace in on this?"

"Nope. Decided a few weeks ago I didn't want you to leave town without a ring on your finger, so I called your dad and asked him if I could marry you."

"It's beautiful." Annie couldn't stop admiring it. It fit her perfectly. "How did you know what size to get?"

He grinned. "I pilfered a ring from your jewelry box."

He was still on one knee in front of her and she pulled his head onto her lap, laying her cheek on top of his head. "I love you, Jimmy. I'll never stop loving you."

He stood up, pulled her up and into his arms and kissed her tenderly.

They walked hand in hand back to his car, both thinking it was the happiest night of their lives.

Little did Annie know that while she was experiencing the best night of her life, Grace was on the other side of town experiencing the worst night of hers.

6

It was the last weekend before finals and Grace sat alone in their dorm room studying. Jimmy had taken Annie out on a special date. Grace had a strong hunch he was going to ask her to marry him. She tried not to feel jealous. Goodness! What would she ever do without her Annie? She was the sister she never had, she loved her dearly and it thrilled her to see her so happy. It was just that she had hoped she would've had her own Jimmy by now. Four years of college, and Grace had only gone on a half dozen dates and been bored silly on all of them.

The most popular fraternity on campus was throwing their annual pre-finals bash. A couple of the girls who lived on their hall begged her to join them. She'd declined, saying she'd better stay in and study. But maybe she could use a break from studying—from feeling sorry for herself because she didn't have her own Jimmy. *What the heck? Why not?*

When she walked down to their room to tell them she'd changed her mind about going, they shrieked with pleasure and poured her a solo cup filled with their famous pre-party punch. Grace wasn't sure what all was in the punch, but after one cup she was feeling pretty jovial.

They continued to sip on their drinks as they decided what to wear. They modeled various outfits for each other. Offering advice on which outfit looked the best. Grace settled on her favorite jeans and a cute halter-top of Annie's. As she inspected herself in the mirror, she had to admit she looked good, she was having a good hair day and she felt pretty.

~ ~

The fraternity house was packed and the music blaring. They'd pushed all the furniture to the sides of the room in order to make a dance floor. Someone had put together a tiki bar in the corner. Grace took it all in, telling herself in all probability this would be her last college party—so she'd better make the most of it.

She spotted Philip Beck standing with a group of his friends. Grace had him in one of her classes, but doubted he'd ever noticed her. But boy, had she noticed him! In her opinion, the best looking guy on campus. He happened to turn just then and caught her staring at him. Emboldened by her pre-party cocktails, she didn't look away. His eyes met hers. After sizing her up from head to toe, he let his eyes return to hers. Neither of them looked away, a staring contest. Grace won. He dropped his gaze and walked away from his group of friends.

Grace looked around for more familiar faces. She was startled when Philip approached her from behind, touching a cold solo cup against her bare shoulder.

"Care for a drink?" he grinned.

"Th-thanks," Grace replied with a nervous stutter, taking it from his hands.

"I know I have you in one of my classes, but I haven't seen you around here . . . is this your first time at the house?"

"Yes." *So he **had** noticed her! Come on, Grace! Think of something witty to say.*

"Having a good time?"

"Yes."

"Are you a senior?"

"Yes."

"Are you always this chatty?" He laughed, and Grace laughed too.

She finally *did* relax and found things to talk about—their majors, which dorm she lived in, where they were from. Their plans after graduation. Friends they had in common—yada, yada.

When he saw her cup was empty, he offered to get her another one. She was already feeling the effects of the first one, but agreed to the second one anyway. He was treating her like she was the only person in the room.

When a slow song came on, he asked her to dance. She jumped at the chance. He pulled her body close and she could feel his attraction.

They stayed out on the dance floor for several songs after the first one. Dancing to all the good dance songs by Earth, Wind and Fire, K.C. the Sunshine Band, and Michael Jackson.

Figured he'd be a great dancer, too.

When another slow song came on, he pulled her close again. He bent his head to her neck, kissed it softly and whispered into her ear how beautiful she was, how good she felt. She felt electrified. She nestled into him, pressed her own lips against his neck. *What was she doing? She had just talked to the guy for the first time!*

There were only a few couples left on the dance floor. Philip suggested they have one more drink and then he'd give her a ride back to her dorm.

She hesitated, "I don't know. I came with some friends . . ." Her gut was telling her it wasn't a good idea.

"Come on, they'll understand. It'll give us more time to talk, to get to know each other a little better."

"That's true. Thanks. But I think I'll pass on another drink."

"Oh, come on! One more drink won't kill you. You've only had a couple."

"But they were strong . . ." She was feeling more than a little buzzed.

He walked back to the fraternity's makeshift Tiki bar and came back with a generously poured drink in each hand.

Grace slipped away to tell her hall-mates, Kim and Amy, that Philip was giving her a ride home.

"Are you sure that's a good idea?" Amy asked.

"I think you've had too much to drink," added Kim.

"I think he might be planning on asking me out. Oh my gosh, can you imagine? *Me*? Going out with Philip Beck?" Grace gushed under her breath. She already knew the outfit she'd borrow from Annie for their first date.

"He's not exactly known as being a nice guy, so be careful."

Grace rolled her eyes. *They're jealous, that's all.*

He led her out to his oh so-cool Trans Am. She waited for him to open the car door for her. But he jumped in, reached over and pushed the door open for her from the inside. She slid in and leaned her head back against the expensive leather seats, sighed with contentment.

He pulled out of the driveway and headed the opposite direction from her dorm.

"Oh! I live in Elizabeth Hall. I'm sorry, I thought I told you."

"You did. I just thought I'd show you my apartment first."

"Umm. No, I better not, maybe tomorrow?" she asked hopefully.

"Come on. I've devoted my entire night to you, I'm not ready to take you home yet." He sounded a tad aggravated and didn't turn the car around.

Would it be so bad to see his apartment? *Come on Grace, don't be such a prude.*

He turned the radio up so loud they couldn't possibly have a conversation. *What happened to wanting to get to know each other a little better?* Not only was it loud, it was acid rock. She hated acid rock. It was giving her a headache.

He didn't hold her hand or try to say anything on the ride to his apartment. When they pulled into the parking lot, he put his arm behind the seat behind her and expertly backed his car into his parking spot. She didn't get out, she shouldn't have agreed to come here, to be alone with him in his apartment. She should insist on him taking her back.

He came around and opened her door. Took her hand and pulled her up. "Come on girl, time's a wasting."

He didn't let go of her hand, unlocking and pushing the door open with his free hand.

He dropped her hand as soon as the door closed behind them.

"Wow, this is nice!" Grace was impressed, "it's so . . . clean." It didn't even look lived in.

"Yep. Old Mabel does a great job keeping the place up."

"You have a maid?"

"Maid, slave. Whatever you want to call her." He laughed.

Grace didn't find it funny.

He pulled her against him, kissing her fully on the lips. Golly, he was a great kisser. She melted into him, responding just as passionately. *What was wrong with her? She was drunk. She needed to get out of there.*

She turned her face away from his, used both hands to push against his muscular chest, but didn't budge him. "I need to get back."

He pulled her tighter against him, turned her face back to his. "Not yet," he murmured against her lips.

He took her hand and pulled her down the hall into his bedroom. He picked her up as easily as if she were a rag doll and laid her on top of his quilt. She was impressed with his strength. He lay on top of her. His body felt good against hers. He started trailing gentle kisses down her neck to the hollow place above her collarbone.

Grace moaned involuntarily. He knew what he was doing, that's for sure.

"That's more like it," he said softly. He returned his lips to hers and she kissed him hungrily back.

The alcohol had gone to her head. *But would it really be so awful to relax and enjoy a little kissing? What harm could a few kisses do?* He lifted her shirt, put his hand under her bra. She tried pushing his hand down. But he was insistent. He was the first guy who'd ever even tried to feel her up. It wasn't right. This wasn't even a real date. She put more pressure on his hand to take it off her breast. He moved his hand down to her waist, expertly unsnapping her jeans. *No way!*

"Stop! I need to go." Grace struggled to get out from under him. "I need to go, NOW!" she repeated louder.

"Not yet." He pulled her shirt and bra completely up to her neck.

"NO! Get *off* of me! STOP!" Grace yelled.

"Shut up! Before someone hears you," he muttered through clenched teeth. He put his hand firmly over her mouth, silencing her. With his other hand he grabbed her wrists and roughly pulled them over her head, coldly assessing her breasts.

"Not bad. I've seen better."

Grace mustered up all her strength to get out from under him, desperately trying to free her mouth, so she could scream for help. He pushed her head harder into the bed. She tried biting his hands.

He took his hand off, but before she could scream, he put his mouth roughly over hers. Not to kiss her but to keep her from screaming. She could feel his teeth cutting into the skin around her mouth.

His grip on her wrists was hurting her.

With his free hand, he roughly unzipped her jeans and started pulling them down. Grace was wild with panic, desperate to stop him. She used every bit of strength trying to twist away from him.

As soon as he got her jeans past her knees he easily pulled them off and flung them aside. He ripped her flimsy underwear, released her wrists just long enough to pull off his own jeans. With her hands finally freed, she scratched his face, pulled on his hair, pushed at him, dug her fingers into the sides of his mouth, trying to get if off of hers, so she could scream for help.

He was able to grab her wrists again and jerk them back above her head.

"Quit being such a tease!" he muttered against her lips, he was breathing heavily from fighting her off.

He finally lifted his lips off of hers and Grace cried out at the pain. Tears dripped down the sides of her face. He collapsed against her, released her wrists and rolled off of her.

She pulled down her shirt, turned away from him. There was no point in screaming for help now. It was done.

She could hear him getting his clothes back on. He flung her jeans over to her.

"I gotta say, I've never had a girl put up a fight like that," he said, without a bit of remorse. "Go ahead and get dressed. I'll drop you back at your dorm. I gotta take a leak, be right out."

As soon as Grace sensed he was gone, she scrambled into her clothes, stuffed her torn panties into her pocket, left the room and stood by the door. She wished her dorm was in walking distance, she'd be gone before he came out. But it was at least ten miles away.

He came out, smelling like toothpaste and soap.

"You drew blood, girl. What the heck is wrong with you?"

She didn't even look at him. She walked out to the car and got in, slamming the door. He took his time getting in and then slowly adjusted the rearview mirror before finally putting it in gear and pulling out.

"Are you gonna give me the silent treatment now? Try and act like you didn't want it?"

Grace continued to stare out the window, ignoring him.

"What'd you expect? You turn a guy on like that, respond like that and then expect him to just turn it off? Huh? Tell you what sweetheart, it doesn't work that way."

"Don't talk. Just drive," Grace said through clenched teeth, still staring out the window.

"Whatever."

Neither of them said another word. He stopped so abruptly in front of her dorm, she almost bashed her head against the dash. She'd barely gotten out and closed the door before he squealed his tires driving away.

Tears streaming down her face, she let herself into the dorm. Muffling her sobs, willing herself not to make a sound, she crept down the hall to her room.

She looked over at Annie sleeping so peacefully. She envied her purity, her sweetness, her resolve to make good choices. Annie would never have allowed herself to be taken to a virtual stranger's apartment. She felt such shame and anger at her stupidity. If only she could have a do-over.

She gingerly laid down on top of the covers, not bothering to undress and risk waking Annie.

A memory verse Grace learned long ago kept haunting her. "*No temptation has seized you except what is common to man. And God IS faithful beyond what you can bear. But when you ARE tempted, He WILL also provide a way of escape.*"

God had provided so many ways of escape that night. She could have escaped by refusing to kiss him on the dance floor, refusing the offer for a ride home, refusing to go into his apartment, rebuffing his disrespectful advances once they were in his apartment. But she didn't, and now she would have to live with the consequences.

Her mother had warned her once that, "temptation always takes you further than you want to go, makes you stay longer than you want to stay and makes you pay more than you want to pay." How Grace wished she couldn't personally attest to the truth of those words.

She didn't even feel worthy to pray. How could she ask God to take away her pain when she had known better?

7

Annie had been disappointed Grace was still out when she got back to their room. She'd been eager to tell her everything. It wasn't like Grace to stay out this late—it must have been one heck of a party. Her news would have to wait until morning.

~ ~

Annie opened her eyes as sunlight filtered through the blinds. She stretched contentedly, savoring the memories of the previous night with Jimmy. Oh, what a night! The best ever.

She knew Grace would be impressed with the effort Jimmy had put into it.

She raised herself up on one elbow to look over at Grace. She was surprised to find Grace lying on top of her quilt with her clothes still on. She must have gotten in really late and didn't want to risk changing into her pj's and waking Annie up. Grace was curled up facing the wall. Annie crept over to look at her, willing her to wake up. Grace looked awful! Her hair was in knots, her eyes puffed up, make-up smeared all over her face. There was dried blood in the corners of her mouth.

Annie was alarmed. She gently touched Grace's shoulder, "Grace?"

Grace slowly woke up. The horror of the night before filling her with shame. She didn't want to look at Annie. She felt like she wanted to die.

"Grace. Look at me."

"I don't want to," Grace mumbled.

"Please, Grace. You're scaring me."

Grace thought she didn't have any tears left in her, yet Annie's concerned voice opened the floodgates. Fresh tears dripped into her hairline, onto her pillow.

Annie reached over and gently turned Grace's face to look at her.

"Oh my gosh, Grace! What *happened* to you?"

Grace turned back to face the wall, curled up into a fetal position, huge wrenching sobs engulfing her.

Annie curled herself against Grace's back, embracing her as best she could. "Shhh, shhh. Grace, it's going to be okay. Whatever happened. It's going to be okay."

"It'll never be okay. Never," Grace moaned.

"Please, Grace. Tell me what happened." She sat up and grabbed a tissue, "Here." When Grace reached for it, Annie saw the bruises.

"Grace! What happened to your wrists? How'd you get those bruises?"

Grace finally sat up, blew her nose. She took a deep breath and without looking Annie in the eye, told her what happened.

Annie remained silent, waited patiently when Grace stopped to wipe away tears and blow her nose. She discretely pulled her engagement ring off and slipped it under her pillow, she couldn't share her news now, not with Grace in this state.

When Grace finally finished her story. Annie took her in her arms and cried with her.

"I'm so sorry, Grace. So sorry this happened to you."

After a few minutes she pulled back, "You have to report this. You can't let him get away with it."

"No!" Grace said frantically. "Please, *please* promise me you won't tell anybody . . . not even Jimmy."

"He might do it to other girls. You might save them."

"It was my own stupid fault for drinking too much and agreeing to go to his apartment with him."

"Don't you dare blame yourself!" Annie said angrily. "'No' means 'No.' Anyone looking at you now, wouldn't question your story. Trust me."

"They would make me look like a whore. A drunk whore. You know they would. He's the big man on campus, I'm a nobody. Everyone would know about it. It would kill my parents."

Annie couldn't deny Grace's logic. It wasn't fair that the monster would get away with it, but he would. It wouldn't matter what the truth was, Grace would be dragged through the mud.

"Oh, Annie! What if I'm pregnant?" Grace moaned and curled back up, her body trembling with fear and grief.

Annie hadn't thought of that. She knelt beside Grace's bed and began praying, "Please Lord, please don't let Grace be pregnant. Please comfort her. Please help her." She didn't know what else to add, but continued to silently plead with Him, tears streaming down her cheeks, too.

Grace threw herself into finishing well. Studied like a mad woman for finals. Submitted dozens of job applications.

Five days after the hideous episode, Grace received two pieces of wonderful news—her period started and she got an offer for a job at a big publishing company in New York City. She would be leaving college on a high note in spite of her wrong choices.

But Grace's college memories would forever be tainted, that one night overshadowing all the wonderful memories.

8

New York City, 1983

The first time she met Chad was at an office Christmas party. He'd only been with the company for a few weeks, but she'd heard all about him—it seemed he'd bewitched every woman in the building. Grace wasn't impressed.

She hated these parties. It was ridiculous that at twenty-four years old, she still got nervous entering a room full of people. She dreaded breaking into conversations and making small talk. She reminded herself of the advice she'd been given—don't worry about trying to be *inter*-*est**ing*** but rather be *interest**ed.*** People loved talking about themselves, she just needed to come armed with the right questions, that's all. She'd be fine.

She glanced around the room, looking for a familiar face. She noticed dear old Dora had roped Chad into a conversation. She smiled inwardly, imagining their conversation. Dora didn't possess the filter that clued her into the fact when she was boring a person senseless. She could talk for hours on end about her cats and physical ailments. You'd be lucky to get a word in edgewise.

She noticed how desperate Chad looked to escape. Maybe she would play the Good Samaritan and rescue him.

She walked over to them, introduced herself to Chad and asked Dora if she would mind if she stole him away for a moment.

She bit back a smile at Chad's overt eagerness to get away.

"Thank you," he whispered as they walked away. "I owe you. Big time."

"I know there's a limit to how many cat stories one can hear. And you looked like you might be reaching that limit," she smiled. "Other than being waylaid by Dora, are you enjoying the party?"

"Not until now," he grinned, taking her in with an appreciative glance. "But it doesn't get much better than being rescued by a beautiful blond."

Most men who dared to look her up and down like that and follow it up with a cheesy comment left her cold. But, for whatever reason, he came off as genuine and she felt flattered by the comment.

They ended up spending most of the night together. They had a lot in common and they laughed together about some of the idiosyncrasies of their co-workers. By the end of the night, he asked her out for their first date.

For the first time in her life she thought she might be falling in love. She'd gone on plenty of dates, but had never so much as given any of them a kiss goodnight.

Chad was her first *real* boyfriend. He was good to her. Always a gentleman, tender, thoughtful, funny, intelligent.

He didn't even try to kiss her on their first date and Grace was relieved. She hadn't kissed anyone since that awful experience her senior year of college.

She worried she might freeze up at their first kiss, but she needn't have. She was plenty attracted to him and thoroughly enjoyed his touch, his kisses. He always wanted to go farther than she allowed, but said he understood her wanting to take it slow. He respected it, said he found it refreshing.

After they'd been dating six months, he surprised her with plans for a romantic weekend in the mountains. She was hesitant to agree to it, she knew what he would expect from her and she wasn't ready to take that step.

Her parents would be horrified she'd even *consider* going away with a man. Not that they'd ever find out. But years of having it drummed into her that "nobody buys the cow when the milk is free" was hard to shake off.

Chad was irritated with her hesitation. His whole demeanor changed.

"I gotta tell you, I expected a little bit of a different response. I put a lot of thought into making this a special weekend."

"I'm sorry. It's just . . . it's just I think we should wait until we're . . ." She couldn't bring herself to say the word "married." She certainly didn't want to be the first one to broach the subject.

"Come on, Grace. I've been patient. It's all paid for and it's non-refundable. It'd be like flushing money down the toilet."

He was making her feel ungrateful and petty. Would it really be such a big deal? It wasn't like she was a virgin, she had Phillip Beck to thank for that. She willed away the guilty memories and horror of that night. Maybe replacing it with a new memory, one filled with genuine love and intimacy would help her put it out of her mind forever.

The bed and breakfast was nestled into the foothills of the Shenandoah Mountains. He wined and dined her, made her feel beautiful and desirable and even treasured.

She held onto a sliver of hope he'd planned the weekend to propose. Even though it had only been six months, he'd told her he loved her—many times. Maybe after a weekend away, he would start talking about a future together.

But if anything, all it ended up doing was opening the door for him to assume she was willing to have sex with him every time they went out. When she tried to stop him and explain how the assumption made her feel, he became aggravated, saying she turned him on, that's all—once he'd experienced "the magic" of having her, he couldn't go back to just kissing.

"Come on," he'd say. "Don't think up stuff to bring us down. It's stupid thinking anyway—of course I 'respect' you." Then he'd smile, pull her into his warm embrace, tell her how beautiful she was and how much he loved her. He continued to spoil her with affection and lavish nights out and she told herself he was right, she *was* being stupid. Would he be investing all this time and money if he wasn't planning on marrying her? It was only the belief that marriage was around the corner that alleviated some of her guilt about sleeping with him.

9

Chad and Grace both loved spending time outdoors. They walked through Central Park even on the coldest of days. When the days started getting warmer, they'd find a sunny spot, lay down a blanket and enjoy picnic lunches.

One day as they lingered over lunch and watched a group of children laughing and playing near them, Grace sighed contentedly, "I can't wait to have babies."

"Really? You've never said anything about kids."

Grace was surprised she'd never shared how much she'd hated being an only child, or how much she loved children. "I've always dreamed of having a big family."

"Hmmm. I can't believe we've never had this conversation, because I'm not even sure I *want* kids."

What? Grace felt like she'd been punched in the gut. She couldn't *imagine* a life without children in it. "Are you serious? Because there is nothing I am *more* sure about."

"I just don't think New York City is the best place to raise kids, and I don't want to live anywhere else."

"I've always thought we . . . I mean I, would live in small house close enough to commute into the city, with a little yard . . ." Grace looked down at her hands, willing herself not to cry.

Chad sat there silently, looking off in the distance. When he finally looked back at Grace, he could see tears trickling down her cheeks, her head still down.

He gently lifted her chin, met her gaze.

"Would it be a deal-breaker?"

"Yes," her throat felt so tight, she could barely speak. "It *would* be a deal-breaker."

He looked into her gorgeous green eyes, made even more spectacular with the sheen of tears; her curls burnished in the bright sunlight. *God, she was gorgeous.* He leaned over and placed his lips on hers, "Then I guess I'll have to think about it, because I don't want to lose you."

She didn't know how to respond, it wasn't enough for Chad to just "think about it." She quietly started packing up to head home.

"Hey! Why the hurry? Let's soak up as much of this sunshine as we can."

"I need some time alone. You can stay, but I'm heading back."

"Well, whatever."

"'Whatever?' That's all you have to say?" Grace responded testily. She walked away before he could add anything else.

As soon as she let herself into her small apartment, she dropped her things and called Annie. When she finished telling her about her and Chad's conversation, she asked for Annie's thoughts.

"You don't want to know what I think."

"Yes, I do. I want you to be honest with me."

"I think it's another red flag."

"*Another* red flag? What are the others?"

"The things I've asked you about before. It's been eight months, why does he still refuse to go to church with you? Why won't he ever go with you to visit your parents? Why did he guilt trip you into having sex with him?"

"He didn't exactly 'guilt trip' me into having sex with him . . . it was the weekend away that kind of opened the door . . ."

"Exactly. He's selfish."

"You've never even met him."

"I don't need to meet him, I can tell just by the things you tell me."

"But we're in love . . . that has to mean something."

"Grace. He's the first boyfriend you've ever had and I think you're turning a blind eye to some of his faults because you like having a boyfriend. Have you been praying about it?"

Grace hadn't. She felt hypocritical praying when she knew she shouldn't be sleeping with him. She heard Annie sigh, "Well, I want you to know, I *am* praying about it and all I see are red flags. Please hang on loosely, Grace."

Grace wanted to steer the subject away from her troubled relationship with Chad. She wanted to talk about Annie and her sweet little family.

"How are Mark and Molly?" Grace asked, making it clear she was done talking about herself and Chad.

Mark was three and Molly was eighteen months; she loved hearing stories about them. She'd only been out to see them one time since she started dating Chad and she missed them.

As if reading Grace's thoughts, Annie suggested she come for a visit. Take a little time away from the city and Chad. Grace promised she would try and work something out soon and Annie promised to keep praying for her.

After their upsetting conversation about children, Grace was disappointed Chad didn't at the very least call to check on her. She'd half expected him to follow her home. It was Saturday, and they had dinner plans. Was he just going to assume all was well and continue on like they hadn't even had the discussion?

Was Annie right about him? Was she ignoring red flags? Was she only turning red flags pink because she wanted a boyfriend? A knock on the door interrupted her thoughts. She looked through her peephole; Chad had cared enough to check up on her after all!

Just as she opened the door to let him in, her friend Cindy opened hers to leave. Cindy stopped dead in her tracks when she spotted Chad. She didn't even acknowledge Grace's presence.

"You must be Chad! I can't believe we've never met. I'm Cindy." She reached out to shake his hand and held on a tad too long.

Cindy was wearing tight jeans and a snug t-shirt. Definitely not dressed for a night out on the town. *Saturday night and she didn't have a date?* Of course, she still looked as fabulous as ever. She couldn't look bad if she tried.

"Pleasure to meet you, Cindy. Grace talks about you all the time."

Cindy kept her gaze locked on Chad. "The pleasure is all mine." She gave him her most brilliant smile, "Well, I'll leave you two love birds alone. I was just stepping out to get some take-out and rent a movie."

"Hey Cindy!" Grace greeted her with feigned enthusiasm, forcing Cindy to acknowledge her. "Don't tell me you don't have a date tonight? Or are you and your man spending the night at your place?"

Cindy finally took her eyes off of Chad and looked at Grace, "Oh, come on Grace, you know I don't have a man."

"I'm sorry, I should have asked is *one* of your men coming over." She knew she sounded catty, but she was unnerved by Cindy's over interest in Chad.

"No. I don't have a date tonight. I'll be all by my lonesome." She pouted prettily.

"That's gotta be a first for you! But sometimes it's good to have a little space." She was eager for Cindy to move along. "So . . . I'll probably see you tomorrow then."

"Wait," Chad broke in. "There's no reason to spend the night alone. Grace and I aren't doing anything special, you could join us."

Grace looked at Chad with daggers in her eyes. How dare him ask Cindy to join them when they'd just discovered something that could end their relationship.

Cindy must have read Grace's look, because she politely refused, "Maybe another time."

As soon as they were alone, Chad could feel Grace's irritation.

"I'm surprised, Grace. I've never seen you act so ungracious."

"You're worried about me being *ungracious* after our conversation this afternoon? An issue big enough to end our . . . us?" She tried to keep the hurt and anger out of her tone, but her eyes were welling up for the second time that day.

"Aw, Grace. I'm sorry. You're right. I wasn't thinking." He pulled her into his arms and kissed the top of her head. "We *do* need this night alone. You caught me off guard when you mentioned having babies. I'm not ready for one *now*, but it doesn't necessarily mean I'll *never* be ready."

Grace stayed still in his arms, resting her head against his chest, but keeping her arms at her sides.

Chad forced her head up and made her look at him. "I'm gonna head home now, get showered up and come get you in an hour. We'll make tonight special. Okay, beautiful?" He gave her a coaxing smile.

She nodded and gave him him a half-hearted kiss good-bye.

They did end up having a nice night. Chad was more affectionate and tender than normal and did his best to cajole her out of her pensive mood. When he suggested going back to his place before taking her home, she knew what he wanted, but she told him she was tired and wanted to go home. For the first time, he didn't try to talk her out of it.

10

Other than co-workers, her neighbor Cindy was the only real friend Grace had made since moving to New York City three years ago. A week after Grace moved in, Cindy invited her over to share a bottle of wine and get to know each other. They clicked immediately.

Cindy was funny and laughed easily. Everyone was drawn to her, especially men. Anytime they went out, Grace watched men's jaws drop when Cindy walked into the room. She had curves in all the right places and wore clothes that showed them off to their best advantage.

She had plenty of men asking her out and Grace loved hearing about all of her dates. Grace thought many of them sounded promising, but she couldn't remember the last time Cindy went out with the same guy twice. She told Grace she'd know when the perfect one came along, in the meantime she'd just enjoy "playing the field."

A few weeks after Chad's chance meeting with Cindy in the hallway, Cindy called and said her date had two extra tickets to one of the most popular plays on Broadway. Would she and Chad be interested in joining them? Chad loved going to shows—Grace knew he'd jump at the chance.

The four of them hit it off beautifully. Grace couldn't imagine why Cindy wasn't falling for her date, Mitch. He was handsome, engaging, and apparently wealthy, and money mattered to Cindy.

The four of them went out the following weekend as well. Before Grace knew it they were hanging out with them regularly.

Grace started feeling twinges of jealousy at the attention Chad gave Cindy. He never failed to compliment her on her how great she looked and she thought he laughed a little too hard at some of her jokes. *Come on,* she'd think, *she's not* ***that*** *funny.*

More and more, they seemed to find ways for the two of them to be having a private conversation, leaving Grace with no choice but to chat with Mitch. A few times she thought she saw them deliberately pressing their knees or shoulders together and letting their fingers touch and linger a little too long.

Was she being paranoid? She didn't want to be jealous and suspicious. When she mentioned to Chad she thought he was paying too much attention to Cindy, he'd rolled his eyes and insisted she was "seeing things."

So why had she been surprised? What hurt most was the sneakiness and deception. Why hadn't he broken it off with her the minute he started having feelings for Cindy? The coward! She'd probably still be in the dark if she hadn't seen them in the restaurant that night.

She'd been away for the weekend, making the obligatory visit to her parents. She decided to come home a day early and surprise Chad. It was past dinnertime, so she'd stopped at one of his favorite restaurants to pick up dessert. She'd spotted them right away, snuggled together in a private booth.

Later on, she thought how odd it was she hadn't confronted them right then, instead, she'd slunk out of the place like *she* was the guilty one—like she'd be interfering on their good time or something. Maybe she'd been afraid of causing a public scene, embarrassed that she'd been deceived. Maybe the shock was too much to process.

But the rage and hurt built up through the night. She didn't sleep a wink, just got angrier by the minute.

She pounded loudly on Chad's door early the following morning and when he cracked open the door she practically knocked him down, pushing violently past him.

"How **could** you? How could you do that to me?" she demanded through clenched teeth.

"What are you talking about? What is **wrong** with you?"

"You and Cindy! **That's** what wrong with me!" she yelled.

"Oh."

"Oh? That's all you have to say??"

"I didn't plan on falling in love with her, Grace . . . it just happened, okay? I'm sorry. We were planning on telling you this week. I didn't want to tell you right before you went to see your parents . . ."

The admission that he *loved* Cindy was a kick in the gut. Before Grace realized what she was doing, she slapped his face with everything she had in her.

At first she thought he might hit her back, he raised his hand as if he might, but instead brought it to his cheek and looked at her disgustedly, "Charming."

She didn't think it possible to get any angrier, yet his look of disgust, coupled with his sarcasm, made her *really* want to hurt him. She gained a new understanding of the term "crimes of passion" and knew she needed to leave.

She started to storm out, but came back and kicked and pushed at his beloved bookcase with all his stupid cassette tapes, trophies and trinkets until the whole thing came crashing down. Breathing heavily, but satisfied with the destruction she'd wrought, she stepped over all the debris and slammed his door so hard it echoed throughout the entire building.

When she got home she called Annie and poured out the whole sad story, crying and sniffling her way through every detail. When she was finished and awaiting Annie's words of sympathy, she heard what sounded suspiciously like laughter.

"Are you laughing???" she asked incredulously.

Annie *was* laughing. She could hardly talk she was laughing so hard. "I'm sorry . . . it's just the whole picture of you pushing down that bookcase . . . and I can just picture you smacking that pretty boy face . . ." She erupted in fresh laughter.

"Well. Gee!" Grace huffed. "If I'd known that being betrayed by a good friend, having my heart ripped out and acting like a wild Tasmanian could put you into fits of laughter, maybe I'd have tried it sooner . . ."

But, suddenly, she was laughing right along with her. It *had* been quite a scene—she could see the humor from an outsider's perspective.

Her heart had just been broken, how could she be crying and laughing at the same time?

When they finally stopped laughing, Annie became serious. "I'm sorry Grace, I really am, but he never deserved you. And Cindy wasn't a true friend. You know I've always thought that. This proves it. Try to be grateful you discovered their true colors when you did."

"How am I going to face going to work tomorrow?" Grace moaned. "He's probably going to tell everyone what a lunatic I acted like. The crazy, scorned woman."

"I think your pride is hurt more than anything else. It was only a matter of time before you opened your eyes and saw him for the selfless brute he is. Hold your head up and ignore him," she advised. "It'll be old news in a matter of days."

"Fat chance. Thank God we don't work in the same department."

"You'll be fine Grace. You're strong. You deserve so much better than that cheating worm. God has someone perfect for you, I know He does."

"I wish I could think like you. I've messed up too much to deserve someone 'perfect' for me."

"There's no such thing as messing up too much to get God's best. And you *can* think like me. I believe with all my heart that God will turn even this mess into something good, because you are *His*, Grace. You could never do anything to make Him love you any less. Deep down, I know you know that."

"I used to know it. But I don't anymore. Maybe I never did," Grace said sadly.

"I think you need a break. Why don't you take a few weeks off and come see me? The kids miss you and I'm desperate to spend some time with you. I bet you could find a great job here. That job was great experience for you, now you can take that experience and probably work anywhere you want. That jerk is going to make it a toxic place to work. You don't need that."

The idea was tempting. Grace didn't want to run from her problems, but she could use the kind of bolstering only Annie could give her. And deep down, she never could picture herself staying in NYC and raising a family here, regardless of how much she loved her job or how much she loved living in the city. She'd already been thinking of ways she could work from home, so she could stay home when she had babies.

"I'll think about it. It's tempting. But for now, I need to go to work and show him he's not going to keep me down."

"That's my girl!"

After they hung up, Grace tried to pray. *"Please God, please forgive me. Please take the hurt and anger away. Help me forgive them. Please show me where I should go, what I should do."*

She didn't feel like her prayers were getting through, but thanked Him for Annie anyway. Thanked Him for giving her a job she'd loved, thanked Him for her health and the health of her parents. She thought of as many things to thank Him for as she could. Her mother always said gratitude was the best way to escape the doldrums. "Count your blessings, name them one by one" and all that. She was willing to try anything.

11

Chad must have alerted Cindy that they'd been found out, because suddenly Cindy was never home. Obviously too much of a coward to apologize to Grace face-to-face. No doubt Chad told her all about her destructive fit of rage, maybe Cindy was afraid of her.

~ ~

A couple of weeks passed without running into Chad. All the chatter about their failed romance had petered out and Grace thought perhaps his ability to rattle her had ebbed as well—until the morning the elevator doors opened and he nonchalantly stepped in.

Her stomach dropped at the sight of him. He didn't even have the decency to look embarrassed or ashamed, instead he took her in slowly, from head to toe, with a derisive grin. How dare him? How could she ever have been attracted to such a jerk? She felt the urge to slap him again; it took real effort to keep her hands at her side.

She couldn't do it. As much as she loved her job, the daily possibility of running into him wasn't worth it. The chance meeting in the elevator was all Grace needed to convince her she needed to make a move. She abruptly stepped to the front of the elevator and put her arm out to keep the doors from closing. She got out and punched the up button for another elevator to take her up to her boss's office. No time like the present.

Thankfully, she wouldn't have to explain the circumstances to him. That was one good thing about an office romance gone bad. Everyone knew everything. She walked slowly down the hall, taking deep breaths and gathering her emotions together. She tapped softly on the door, waiting to be beckoned in.

She would miss her boss. It saddened her to think she might never again work for someone as kind and affirming as he'd always been.

He greeted her with a warm smile, leaned back in his office chair, hands clasped behind his head, ready to listen. "To what do I owe the pleasure?"

"I can't work here any longer." She hadn't meant to break it that quickly. But why stumble through unnecessary pleasantries? "I'm sure I don't need to fill you in on all the lurid details, but it's getting in the way of my work, it's not fair to you or anyone else for my head not to be in the game."

"Understandable. But I don't want to lose you, you're a great asset and one my most trusted editors. I'm willing to give you as much time off as you need. Paid."

Grace hadn't expected such a sympathetic and generous offer. She felt her throat tighten with emotion.

"I don't think a break is going to do it," she finally answered. "I've put a lot of thought into it and I'm putting in my resignation." Her tone was resolute.

She could tell her boss was genuinely disappointed.

"Is there anything I can do to change your mind? Why don't you see how you feel after a few weeks off? Then we'll talk."

She sadly shook her head. She knew she wasn't going to change her mind. She'd spent the last few weeks thinking long and hard about it, and as much as she loved being a part of the publishing world, she decided she needed to do something different for a while.

She promised she would stay however long it took to finish the projects she'd started.

⁓ ⁓

She'd begged her co-workers not to make a big deal of her leaving. Some of them knew she'd been thinking of ways to cut back on her hours even before her messy break-up with Chad. She wanted to leave with as little drama as possible. Most of them understood.

She didn't tell anyone the exact day she was leaving, she just stayed late that day and packed up her handful of belongings out of her tiny office.

She didn't have any doubts she was making the right decision and even felt a little excitement about starting the next chapter of her life. Like Annie said, she *was* marketable. Who knew what else was out there?

Driving home she considered what her next move should be. Maybe she should sublet her apartment and move back in with her parents until she found a new job. She knew nothing would make them happier than to have their baby girl back under their roof, even if only for a short while.

She hadn't talked to Annie since she'd made her decision to resign. She wished they could talk more, but the long distance phone calls got expensive. She couldn't wait to call her and tell how *good* she felt about her decision, not doubting for a minute it was the right one.

As soon as Grace let herself into her apartment and set her small box of belongings on the table she dialed Annie's number.

"Guess what, Annie? Today was my last day, I said all my good-bye's and . . ."

Before she could finish, Annie interrupted. "OH. MY. GOSH!" she began excitedly. "You are ***not*** going to ***believe*** this! I swear it's a Divine Appointment."

Grace couldn't help but smile at Annie's enthusiasm.

"Less than an *hour* ago, my mom called and asked me if I had any friends that might be interested in a nanny position. Of course, ***you*** were the first person that came to mind. My mom thought you'd be perfect, too. I had a strong hunch you were going to quit your job, but I didn't know for sure, or how soon. And then, ***today*** you tell me this is your last day! Incredible! You'd just be watching *one* little girl, Grace. It would be so easy. You love kids. I bet you could even find some editing jobs you could do on the side. Please, *please* say you'll consider it."

"Why do they need a nanny?"

"It's such a sad story, Grace! The mother died in a car accident when the baby was only three months old. It was my mom's friend's only daughter. I guess the husband was so distraught after the accident he couldn't care for the baby, so the grandmother, my mom's friend, pretty much raised her until now. She didn't think it was fair to the dad or the baby to live in separate houses and insisted the baby move back with her dad. He works full time and needs someone to care for her during the day."

Surprisingly, Grace was intrigued by the story, and by the position. It sounded like it might be the perfect job until she decided what she ultimately wanted to do.

"So the dad would be my new boss. He'll probably want to interview me."

"I would think so."

"If I get bad vibes, I won't do it. I don't want some lonely widower thinking he's gonna get anything more than a nanny."

"Trust me, if my mom didn't think this guy was on the up and up, she wouldn't have asked if I had any friends interested in the job. I even met him once and he seemed nice enough. Oh, Grace! Could you imagine how wonderful it would be to live in the same town? I miss you so much."

"It *would* be wonderful. Goodness, I mean, what do I have to lose? I'll come and interview for it."

"Yesssss!!!" Annie punched her fist in the air. "God is so good. I *know* it's gonna work out. There is no such thing as coincidences. The ***very*** day you quit is the ***very*** day this job opportunity came up, in the ***very*** same city I live in!"

It was difficult not to let Annie's enthusiasm rub off on Grace.

"Annie, don't be so sure. He may not like me, or I might not like him, or . . . well anything can happen. I'm willing to come and interview, but I don't want you to get your hopes up too high."

~ ~

It didn't take long for Grace to move out of her apartment. She left most of her furniture. The only piece she took with her was the small writing desk her parents had given her when she graduated from college. She was able to fit all her clothes, books, pictures, linens and even her desk into her small, hatchback Ford Pinto.

12

Just as she knew they would be, her parents were thrilled when Grace told them she would be spending a few days with them before setting out on the long drive to Eastbrook, Ohio, where she'd be interviewing for the nanny position.

Really, other than the summer after high school, Grace hadn't been home much. Annie's parents had moved to Cincinnati their freshman year of college and every summer Annie's dad hired Grace to work in his shop. Grace's parents didn't have the means to help her with her college expenses, so they were thrilled she was able to make money during her summer breaks.

Then after graduating, she headed straight to her job in New York. It was no wonder they wanted to jump for joy when Grace told them she'd be spending a few days with them.

Her parents were excited about her new job opportunity, too. They knew Annie was good for Grace, and they thought a new job in the same small town Annie lived in was just what Grace needed, even if it ended up only being temporary.

As Grace turned down the familiar lane, she was reminded of all the fun memories she and Annie made in high school. All those nights they'd spent at each other's houses, talking and laughing into the wee hours of the night. How she wished her life was as carefree now as it'd been then.

Grace had lived in the same home, on this same little street her whole life. Her parents never aspired for anything more. They were committed not to "chase after the things of this world." They couldn't relate to people always striving for bigger and better things. So many of the houses on their street had fallen into disrepair, but her father was a stickler for keeping a nice lawn and keeping the trees and shrubs beautifully trimmed up. One of her mother's few hobbies was gardening, and her green thumb created an abundance of color and beauty throughout every season.

As her tires crunched over the gravel driveway, she wasn't surprised to see both her parents come out to greet her. They appeared full of trepidation, unsure of how to handle her broken heart.

They'd known all about Chad, and even though he'd always had an excuse not to accompany her on her visits, she had them convinced that when they did finally meet him, they would love him. Of course, their biggest concern was his faith, or lack thereof. It was always their first question, "how deep is his faith?" Grace told them they didn't talk about it much, but she knew he believed in God . . . so for *once*, could they please just trust her and not judge him before they even met him?

Remembering, Grace chided herself for how prickly she'd acted. They'd been justifiably concerned. She knew they only wanted the best for her and faithfully prayed for her. Who knows? Maybe they had "prayed" Cindy into the picture.

Looking at them now, Grace was overwhelmed with thankfulness for their unconditional love. Where would she be without them? She felt like a baby chick being clucked over. Her father predictably telling her she got more beautiful every time he saw her and her mother worriedly adding she was getting too skinny. Her mother was forever trying to fatten her up.

She resolved not to be impatient with them, but instead appreciate them for who they were. Right now she was craving a little bit of the simple goodness and purity that described their lives. They'd never visited her in New York. She'd never wanted them to. In fact, she'd wanted them to know as little as possible about her life there, because she knew they would find it worrisome.

After eating a delicious home cooked meal and being filled in on all the latest news about friends and family, Grace helped her mother clean up and then begged off any further catching up until the following day.

She appreciated their carefulness in avoiding any painful conversations about what had happened between her and Chad. They knew she would talk about it when she was ready, and they didn't pry.

They understood she was physically and emotionally spent and encouraged her to get cozy and curl up with a good book.

Her mother hadn't changed a thing about her bedroom since she was a little girl. Grace remembered wanting a white, four-poster canopied bed more than anything in the world and they'd surprised her with it on her eighth birthday.

As she looked around, she realized for the first time how much they must have sacrificed in order to buy her the beautiful white bedroom set. They'd always struggled to make ends meet, never buying anything for themselves and shunning modern conveniences. Her home and her old-fashioned parents used to embarrass her, and other than Annie, she'd avoided bringing many friends home with her.

She climbed into her crisp, clean sheets, dried out on the line. Oh, how she missed that smell!

She tried to get lost in her novel, but couldn't. She couldn't stop ruminating about Chad and Cindy. It wasn't *fair* for them to be so happy after hurting her so deeply. She couldn't stop hoping bad things would happen to them. She knew her unwillingness to forgive was only hurting herself. She vowed to get beyond it. She knew it would take time, but she *would* get there.

She understood why she was feeling emotionally bereft, but this acute feeling of spiritual emptiness was new. Witnessing her parents' simple contentment in what little they had and listening to Annie talk so assuredly about God being in control made her yearn for what they had. When had she stopped talking to Him, stopped believing He loved her? Was it guilt? Was it fear she would never stop being punished for her wrong decisions?

Was she only seeking His love and direction now because her heart had been broken and she didn't have anyone else to turn to? Was it God's way of drawing her back to Him?

Please Lord, she whispered, *please forgive me for going my own way, for allowing myself to be conformed to the world, rather than set apart to live by Your standards. I need to know You still love me. I know I don't deserve it, but please give me a sign You are still with me. I want to trust You with all my heart, I don't want to lean on my own understanding. I need You to direct my path.*

After hours of tossing and turning she finally gave up on sleep and decided to get up and scrounge up something to eat. She pulled on her old threadbare bathrobe and crept down the hall to the kitchen. As she passed the living room she decided to peruse some of her parent's books. They were avid readers, she'd give them that. One entire wall of their living room was shelved and filled with books. Not anything particularly interesting, but still, maybe a boring theology book would be just the ticket to help her sleep. As she skimmed through the titles to see if any caught her eye, her eyes were drawn up to the top shelf. An ancient Bible was up there, probably one that listed all the births and deaths through the years.

She had to pull the ottoman over to help her reach it. The dust on it was thick, obviously not a Bible they looked at much. As Grace pulled it down, a folded slip of notepaper fell out. Curious, Grace unfolded it. It was hand written in small cursive handwriting and dated two days after her birthday.

Her hands started to shake as she read it, *"My sweet baby, I don't know as I write this if you will ever read it, but I pray that someday, when the time is right, your parents will allow you this small glimpse into my heart . . ."*

Grace's heart raced and she got goose bumps. What did this mean? Could it mean Grace was adopted and had never been told? Why else would her parents have this? It would certainly explain why Grace didn't look anything like anyone in the family.

Even if her parents came up with some other explanation as to why they had this, Grace's heart went out to the person who'd written it. She was touched by the words. What a wonder it would be if she *had* been adopted. If she had a birth mother she'd never known about that had been praying for her *every* day of her life.

She knew she couldn't wait until morning to find out the story behind it. With the paper in hand, she walked down the hallway to her parent's room and softly knocked. Her mother beckoned her in, reaching to turn on the bedside lamp.

Grace didn't say a word, just passed the note to her mother. As soon as her mother saw what it was, she blanched. She didn't need to read it. Her eyes filled with tears; she struggled to speak.

"I was afraid," her mother whispered, "I was afraid if you ever found out you were adopted, you would want to meet her and then, once you met her, you wouldn't want to be our little girl anymore."

Grace's heart went out to her mother, looking so small in her big bed with the notepaper clutched in her hand. She went and knelt beside the bed, took her mother's free hand in hers. Looking earnestly into her eyes, she asked, "How could you ever believe I'd consider anyone but you as my mother?"

"I've followed up on her all these years, she has other children now and, well, you're all we have . . ."

"But, didn't you promise her you'd give me this prayer?" Grace interrupted.

"I never promised. And since I knew she had to be talked into giving you up in the first place I thought she'd try to take you away from us if she could. I couldn't risk it."

Grace continued to stare at her mom, watched her lower her eyes, watched the tears slip down her cheeks. She looked pitiful. Grace couldn't be angry with her. She looked over at her dad, who looked intently back at her, silently pleading with her to understand.

"Can you tell me about her?" Grace asked quietly.

Her parents looked at each other. Her father took her mother's hand and nodded encouragingly.

"She named you. She wanted you to be called Grace because she said she'd received so much grace. You look a little bit like her. You have her same curly hair," her mother said softly. "She's married to a doctor and has four other children. She lives in the same small Kentucky town you were born in. I've never had any communication with her. That's all I know."

"Wow," Grace breathed out. "So I have four half brothers and sisters I never knew about. It's kind of exciting actually. She *must* want to meet me, at least this prayer makes me think that."

"Well, she wrote it a long time ago. She was just a young teenager. She's married now, with all those children. Her life is full, she might not welcome something that would rock it."

As much as Grace hated to admit it, she knew her mother was right. She couldn't just drop into her birth mother's life. She would contact her, and as much as it would hurt Grace to be kept away, she would have to honor her wishes, even if it meant never meeting her *or* her half brothers and sisters.

"How about my real dad? Do you know anything about him?"

"Nothing," her mother answered. "He was never mentioned, his name never appeared on anything we were given, and thankfully, he never came forward."

Grace's mother seemed torn about adding another detail. Was it her imagination or was her father silently prompting her to say more? Grace waited to see if her mother wanted to add anything, when she didn't, she gently extracted the notepaper from her mother's hand. She kissed her soft cheek before standing up. She took time to gather her thoughts before she spoke.

"I want you to know I could never think of anyone else as my parents. You have raised me and loved me, and sacrificed for me. You've also told me my whole life that everything happens for a reason, so there must be a *reason* I got up in the middle of the night, reached for that old Bible and this prayer fell out. And for whatever reason, reading it made me feel remembered. It made me believe God sees me in this sad and lonely place I'm in. I *want* to believe God led me to find it. To discover there is someone out there faithfully praying for me. It just gave me a kind of . . . boost, I guess."

Her parents ached for her, oh, how they hated to see their little girl hurting.

"We pray for you," her mom replied defensively. "We've *always* prayed for you."

Grace impulsively sat on the edge of the bed and pulled her mother close.

"Be happy for me Mother. I will always be your daughter. I've been so down, so lost and lonely, uncertain about what I should do next. I've prayed more in these last few days than I have in a decade. I've been pleading with God to show me the way I should go. I thought marriage and babies were right around the corner, and then my heart got broken and now . . . this." She held up the notepaper. "It's given me hope that, just like Annie is always telling me, God has plans for me, plans to prosper me and not to hurt me. Maybe I'm *meant* to meet my birth mother."

Grace stood back up, smiling gently down at her beloved parents. She blew them a kiss before closing the door and returning to her room.

She read and re-read the prayer her young teenage mother had written and finally fell asleep with it on her chest.

She resolved to enjoy her short stay with her parents, to love on them like they deserved.

When it came time for her to leave, she left with a much lighter heart. She felt closer to God than she'd felt since she was a little girl. She was excited to be on the road with the promise of spending time with her best friend and Lord willing, a new job.

13

Eastbrook, 1984

Grace arrived in Eastbrook several hours before her scheduled meeting with her prospective employer. She had time to explore the town. She slowly drove down the tree lined streets, admired the older homes, the big front porches. So much charm. It was an unusually warm evening for late fall, there were lots of people out strolling hand in hand, pushing baby strollers and following behind small children on bikes. A perfect slice of small town Americana. What a difference from New York City!

She looked at her watch. She still had over an hour before her interview. She remembered seeing a coffee shop on Main Street and decided she'd backtrack and have a cup of coffee.

As she approached the door a man was coming out and held the door for her. Grace looked at him, nodding her thanks.

He stopped dead in his tracks, still holding the door, staring into her eyes, not saying a word. It was unsettling, and she couldn't help but stare back, looking into the darkest brown, almost black eyes she'd ever seen. He was take-your-breath away handsome. Her face started to redden as he continued to hold her gaze.

"Your eyes," he finally spoke. "They're beautiful . . . they remind me of my daughter's."

"Uh . . . thanks," she said, taken aback at the compliment. Her eyes dropped involuntarily to his ring finger. Married. *Figured. The snake.*

"Excuse me," Grace said coldly, "but if you don't mind, I'd like to go in and get a coffee."

He hesitated just a moment and she impatiently slipped around him.

Matt stood stunned, still holding the door. *Did the silly woman think I was trying to hit on her?* He wasn't used to cold responses from women. He was used to girls coming on to *him*, not the other way around. He got halfway to his car and decided he'd go back and set her straight.

He strode back in and spotted her seated in the corner. She looked up as he approached, those beautiful green eyes regarding him coolly, "Yes?"

"I wanted you to know, just because I paid you a compliment, doesn't mean I was hitting on you. That's not exactly my style." He spoke succinctly, without a smile. He wanted to add that her whole look wasn't his style, but he didn't.

"I'm sure your wife will be happy to know that that isn't 'your style.'"

Her rejoinder appeared to aggravate him even more. His jaw tightened.

"For your information . . ." He stopped mid-sentence, turned on his heel and walked out.

Grace ordered her coffee and pulled a book out of her bag. She couldn't concentrate. The words swam in front of her. That man had unnerved her. What a pompous jerk. Probably so used to girls falling all over themselves for him he couldn't handle being rebuffed.

She gathered up her things and headed back to her car. She traversed the few blocks back to the little home she'd found earlier. An adorable cape cod with a huge front porch with a porch swing.

She knocked once. Heard steps on the hardwood floor.

The door opened and she was face to face with the "pompous jerk" from the diner.

"No way!" He threw back his head and laughed. "*You're* Grace?"

"Yes," she answered quietly. Had she ruined her chance of getting the job? Acting so prickly when she noticed he was married? So he wasn't *really* married. He just wasn't over losing his wife, obviously couldn't bring himself to remove his wedding ring.

She wished she hadn't taken such care to *look* the part of a nanny. She had slicked her hair back into a tight bun and didn't have a speck of make-up on. She'd worn sensible shoes, boring dress slacks and a loose cardigan sweater over a turtleneck.

"I'm Matt. Obviously. But it's nice to *officially* meet you." He offered her his hand, and his warm clasp gave her tingles right down to her toes."Could I get you something to drink? A glass of water or a soda?"

"Water sounds great." Her nervousness had made her feel parched.

"Water it is." He turned and motioned for her to follow him into the kitchen. She couldn't help but notice the pictures of his beautiful wife. A large wedding picture hung in the hallway, grinning faces of marital bliss. There was another shot of the two of them on a beach somewhere.

In the kitchen, he pulled out a chair for her, then took a glass out of the cupboard. "Would you like ice?"

"Yes, please."

He filled her glass with ice and water, handed it to her and then pulled out a chair for himself, resting his ankle comfortably on his opposite knee.

"I'm ashamed to admit it, but I didn't come up with anything specific to ask you about. You came so highly recommended, I was tempted to sign you on sight unseen. But then I decided maybe I *should* meet you, in case I got some weird vibes about you or something."

"But you aren't?" Grace asked tentatively, ". . . getting any 'weird vibes' about me?" How odd she had echoed those same thoughts to Annie about *him*.

Matt laughed. "Nope, no weird vibes. And when you see Ella, you'll realize I wasn't laying some cheesy line on you, either. The more I look at you, the more uncanny it is. Your eyes are exactly the same color and shape as hers. So unless you're getting some weird vibes about me, the job is yours."

"I'm sorry for the way I acted at the coffee shop, I just kind of thought you were, um, well . . ." She could feel her face starting to redden again, "But anyway, no . . .I'm not feeling any weird vibes," she smiled.

No weird vibes, only an undeniable attraction.

"You don't need to apologize. After I cooled down, I could see if from your perspective. So, do you have any questions for me?"

"No." She *did* have questions, but she'd gotten so flustered she'd forgotten what they were.

"Not anything about the hours or the pay? I know you have a copy of the basic stuff, but was there anything you wanted to ask about? Anything you'd like to change? It's not written in stone."

"No, I found everything satisfactory." *Satisfactory? She sounded like a nerd.*

"Well then, are you ready to meet Ella? My mother-in-law Kate is upstairs with her."

He walked over to the bottom of the stairs and called up. "Kate? You and Ella want to come down and meet Grace?"

Grace looked up and saw Kate at the top of the stairs, scooping Ella up before she descended. Ella had a well-worn, obviously well loved rag doll clutched tightly in her arms. Kate gently set her down but Ella clung to Kate's legs, turning shyly to peek at Grace.

Matt watched Grace closely. He knew she wouldn't be able to deny what he'd said about Ella's eyes.

Grace squatted down to Ella's height. As soon as Ella turned to face Grace, Matt could see the shock of recognition. Those same unusually green eyes, slightly tilted up, just like hers.

"Hi Ella." She smiled warmly. "Do you have a name for your baby?"

"Baby," Ella answered shyly.

"Your baby's name is 'Baby'?

Ella nodded.

"I love it," Grace answered enthusiastically, which finally got a smile from Ella.

"And this is my mother-in-law Kate . . ."

Grace stood back up and Kate warmly shook her hand. "Annie has told me so much about you! It's great to finally meet you."

Kate couldn't stop staring at Grace. She got goose bumps . . . this couldn't be *the* Grace could it? No. Of course not! She remembered Eva telling them the couple that adopted Faith's twin were from some small town in upstate New York. She was sure Annie said Grace was from New York City. She was just a girl named Grace that bore a very faint resemblance to Faith.

Thinking of Faith gave her a fresh stab of pain. She missed her only daughter more than she could have imagined. She would never get over losing her so tragically.

Kate watched Grace interacting with Ella. Any worries about hiring Grace for the job evaporated. She could tell Grace was a natural with children.

Kate and Matt together filled Grace in on all the pertinent details of what her job would entail. When there was nothing else to add, Grace stood up and thanked them for being so thorough, told them she thought everything would work out perfectly.

She would be starting the following Monday. She gave them Annie's phone number, just in case they thought of anything else. Matt showed her to the door and just like that, Grace was once again employed.

Grace drove the short distance to Annie and Jimmy's house. She'd be staying with them until she could find a place of her own.

As soon as Annie opened the door, Grace blurted out, "Why didn't you tell me he was drop-dead gorgeous?"

Annie giggled, "I didn't want to intimidate you. Did you get the job?"

"I almost blew it!" Grace told her about running into Matt at the diner.

"That is *too* funny! But I'm sure he was blown away by your beauty. You'd probably have gotten the job on your looks alone."

"My looks? Are you kidding? Look at me! I thought I should try and *look* like a nanny and I look as ugly as sin."

Annie couldn't help but laugh. "You've looked better, but you could never look ugly."

"But his line about my eyes was genuine. Have you ever seen Ella? I have to admit, her eyes are just like mine, same color, everything."

"I've never seen the baby, and I only met Matt just the one time. He's kind of hard to forget."

"If possible, his wife was even more gorgeous than he is. There are pictures of her all over the house."

"It's awful what happened to her," Annie said softly. "Poor guy. Poor Ella."

"I know. I'm sure no one could ever take her place," Grace added wistfully.

"You never know, maybe he'll fall in love with you."

"I'm sure there's no chance of that happening. Plus, I don't think I'd even want to spend the rest of my life living in some woman's shadow, never being able to measure up."

"Never say never!" Annie said teasingly. She reached out and impulsively hugged Grace. "I am so excited for you!"

Grace had to admit, she was excited too. Now she just needed to find a place to live. But it was on Annie's prayer list, so she had little doubt God would lead her to the perfect place.

14

Monday morning came, and Grace pulled up right on time. She'd taken extra care getting ready that morning. She didn't want Matt thinking she was trying to impress him, yet she still wanted to look good. She settled on wearing her most flattering jeans and put on just enough make-up to play up her best features without making herself look too made up.

It took a few minutes before Matt came to the door. He was barefoot, his shirt unbuttoned and his tie looped around his neck.

"I'm sorry. Seems I'm always running late. Ella's still sleeping. There's coffee if you want some. I'll be right down."

Grace scrounged around for a cup and poured herself some coffee. She held the warm mug in both hands, taking in the general unkemptness of the kitchen. Dishes were piled in the sink. There was a basket of dirty clothes sitting on the floor. Crumbs were on the table. She wondered if she was supposed to be the maid too. Not that it would be any trouble.

In minutes Matt was back. Suit coat on, tie tied, his thick hair neatly combed. She couldn't help but admire him or keep from noticing how good he smelled.

"Sorry about the mess. The weekends always get away from me." He smiled as she looked around. "Please don't worry about cleaning up, I'll have plenty of time to get 'er done tonight after I put Ella to bed." He brushed some crumbs off a chair before sitting down, continuing to talk as he bent down to tie his laces. "Anyway, Kate, God bless her, has written down everything you need to know, down to the last detail. What Ella usually eats for breakfast and lunch, what time she takes a nap, games she likes to play . . . the whole nine yards. Really sorry to rush off like this. Kate wrote both my work number and her phone number down in case you have any questions. I'll try and give you a ring at some point today."

He stood back up, grabbed his keys off the counter, apologized again for having to rush off. The door closed behind him before Grace realized she hadn't uttered one word.

She looked down at her watch. She had more than an hour before Ella was due to wake up. She hadn't planned on having time on her hands. She wandered into the living room and flipped on the TV, nothing but boring morning talk shows. She flipped it back off.

She tiptoed into Ella's room to check on her. She couldn't help but stare, smiling at the sweet sight of the beautiful toddler sleeping, one pudgy arm flung carelessly above her head.

She looked around the room, admiring how tastefully it was decorated. The walls were painted a soft pink. There was a cozy white rocking chair in the corner, padded with pink-flecked material. A framed picture of Faith holding Ella as a newborn sat on the small table next to the chair. Grace studied it. Faith was gazing rapturously down at her newborn baby, her hand gently clasping one of Ella's tiny hands. The shiny curtain of Faith's auburn hair covered half her face. She looked like a model. Matt's heart must hurt every time he looked at it.

Grace was a little apprehensive about Ella waking up and discovering her dad and grandmother weren't there. She thought she'd done a fairly good job of winning her over Wednesday night. But that was Wednesday and today was Monday. A long time for a child.

She snuck back out and wandered through the rest of the house. She picked up toys and straightened pillows. What was she supposed to do with the extra time? She went into the kitchen, washed the dishes, wiped down the counters, swept up the crumbs. It took all of about fifteen minutes. She looked at the basket of clothes, picked it up and took it down to the basement where she knew they must have a washer and dryer. As she walked back up the stairs, she heard Ella calling, "Gamma, Gamma!"

Kate hurried up the stairs to get her. "Hey, Ella," she greeted her gently, reaching to pick her up.

"No!" Ella plopped back down. "Gamma!" Her eyes filled with tears and Grace's heart sunk with the realization it wasn't going to be as easy as she'd hoped.

She tried to distract Ella with questions. Where was Baby? Would she help Grace find her? Would she show her where her books were?

At the mention of Baby, Ella looked around, lifting her blankets and finally discovering Baby tucked behind the crib's bumper pad.

She lifted her triumphantly, "Here Baby is!" She smiled at Grace through her tears and handed her the rag doll.

Grace embraced the doll like she was a real baby, talking to her about what they were going to do that day. "How 'bout Ella and I take you for a walk? Would you like that, Baby?"

The entire time she "talked" to the doll, Ella studied her curiously. Finally, she stood back up and reached for Grace, seeming to accept that Grace was the only one there.

After changing her, Grace carried her downstairs and put her in her highchair. Ella continued to watch her intently. Grace kept up a steady conversation. Ella didn't say a word but obediently ate her breakfast and let Grace clean her up. It was a beautiful day, Grace wanted to make the most of it—take Ella for a walk and enjoy the sunshine.

All in all, they had a good day together. A better start than Grace had hoped. When Matt walked in Ella was on her lap and she was reading her a book.

As soon as Ella heard Matt, she scrambled down and ran to him. Matt scooped her up, hugging and kissing her neck until Ella screamed with giggles. Grace stood, silently admiring the tender picture the two of them made.

Ella turned in Matt's arms and pointed at Grace, "Gwace."

Matt smiled. "It looks like it went well. Sorry I didn't get a chance to call you. I was busy in meetings all day."

"That's okay. We did fine, didn't we, Ella? We went for a walk, read some books, played some games . . ."

Grace couldn't think of anything else to add, and Matt seemed equally at a loss for words. When she'd shown up that morning, Matt had been surprised how different she looked. For the "interview" her hair was pinned up into a ridiculous looking bun and a large, ugly cardigan sweater hid her figure. Today she had her curly blond hair pulled up into a loose ponytail. She had on faded jeans and a pink t-shirt.

When she turned to put her jacket on he couldn't help but notice how her jeans hugged her curves. He couldn't remember the last time he'd noticed a pretty woman. He'd forgotten what the stirrings of attraction even felt like.

Grace walked over to the table where she'd left her keys, "Okay. I'll see you tomorrow then. Bye, Ella." She wanted to give Ella a kiss on the cheek, but thought it too familiar a gesture after just one day.

It was awkward, saying so little. She needed to get over this awkwardness. He was a great looking guy, so what? He was just a man, and her boss to boot.

15

As the days went by, it got easier to tell Matt about their day. She shared funny "Ella stories" with him, and he always laughed appreciatively.

Grace noticed Matt brought home fast food most nights for himself and Ella. She knew Matt's culinary skills were minimal. From the looks of the refrigerator and pantry it looked like their dinners mainly consisted of Chef Boyardi Spaghettio's and canned fruit and vegetables.

Grace wanted to be useful during Ella's naptime. It gave her over an hour of time to herself. She would offer to have dinner ready when Matt came home. It would be no big deal.

She was hesitant to suggest it, not wanting him to think she was planning on horning in on their dinnertime. She would make it clear she would eat her own dinner at Annie and Jimmy's.

At first Matt said it would be asking too much. She already did too much. He never expected her to do the things around the house that she did. But Grace was insistent. She had time on her hands—it would give her something to do. She enjoyed it. Really. She wrote out a grocery list for him. If he could pick up the things she needed, she would fix dinner for them Monday night.

Grace had the table set and dinner ready when Matt walked in the door. She immediately pulled on her jacket, making it clear she wasn't planning on staying for dinner. Matt implored her to join them but, of course, she politely declined.

The next morning he gushed about how good dinner had been. He was easy to please and couldn't be more grateful. It made her effort all the more gratifying.

Though Grace thought she made the grocery list specific enough, Matt often got the wrong thing, obviously not accustomed to grocery shopping. After about three weeks, Grace offered to do the shopping.

"I love having a reason to get out of the house, and it would be good for Ella."

"If you're sure . . ." Matt didn't want Grace to think he was taking advantage of her. He sure didn't want to lose her. In the few months she'd been with them, she'd become invaluable.

"I'm sure. I'll save the receipts. You can tack it on to my paycheck at the end of the month."

Every time she took Ella out, people went on and on about how cute "her" little girl was. Grace eventually tired of telling them she was only the nanny. She just thanked them.

The clerk in the grocery store was particularly enchanted with Ella's curls and big green eyes. When they were checking out she looked at Ella and said, "you sure do look like your Momma."

Ella's eyes widened, "You can see Momma? In Heaven?"

The clerk looked at Grace, "I'm sorry. I just assumed you were her mother. You must be an Aunt?"

"Nope. No relation. But I'm flattered. Thank you!"

Ella listened carefully to every word. She understood the clerk thought Grace was her mother. As Grace lifted her out of the cart to put her in her car seat she put her soft pudgy hand gently on Grace's cheek. "Momma."

"No honey, I'm not your Momma. I'm just Grace," she said as she nuzzled her neck.

"Momma Gwace."

"No Ella, just Grace."

"Momma Gwace," Ella insisted more firmly.

Grace didn't answer. Once Ella got on to something, it was difficult to distract her. Somehow she had gotten it into her little head she could have two Mommas. Momma Gwace here, and her other Momma in Heaven. Grace whispered a prayer she'd forget about it by the time they got home.

When Matt got home that night and picked Ella up she turned in his arms and pointed at Grace, "Momma Gwace,"

Grace blushed to the roots of her hair, mortified Matt would think she'd asked Ella to call her Momma. She was quick to jump in and explain it to him.

"A clerk at the grocery store thought I was her mom. For some reason it put the idea in Ella's head that I was her mom, too. I told her I wasn't, but she insisted. I was hoping she'd forget about it . . ."

"Don't worry about it. I can see how people would mistake you for her mom. It must happen all the time."

Grace wanted his help, "See Ella? I'm just Grace."

"Momma Gwace."

Matt laughed and put her down, without correcting her. He apparently didn't see it as something Grace should be too concerned about, or that it took anything away from Faith.

"Ella did make an interesting observation as we were driving," Grace added with a laughing twinkle in her eye. "She said, she was 'glad the idiots stayed home, cuz when daddy drives the idiots make him mad.'"

Matt't booming laughter that Grace was learning to love to much, made her laugh out loud, too.

"Busted," Matt finally got out. "I guess I need to be a little more aware of what little eyes and ears are taking in."

It felt so good to laugh with Matt. One of the things Grace enjoyed the most about him was how easily he laughed.

She knelt to embrace Ella before she left, "See you in the morning, sweet girl."

"Bye, Momma Gwace."

Regardless of how many times Grace told her she wasn't her Momma, Ella persisted and from that day forward she called Grace "Momma Gwace."

16

Matt was surprised how much he looked forward to coming home to Grace and Ella. His attraction to Grace grew by the day. He was so physically aware of her that he took extra care to avoid touching her, allowing a wide berth when she walked by to ensure they never even accidentally touched.

He found himself thinking about her throughout the day, smiling to himself as he remembered what a kick she got out of Ella. Sometimes she'd be laughing so hard as she related the stories she could barely get the words out. Ella *was* quite a little character.

They talked about their shared faith, books and movies they'd liked and even politics. They found themselves agreeing on almost everything.

She started opening up more about her life, too. She talked about how much she had loved her job in New York. When Matt asked why she left, she looked away and said there were several reasons, but she didn't elaborate and he didn't press her.

She told him she was an only child, how much she'd always wished she had brothers and sisters—"But guess what? I just found out I *do* have brothers *and* sisters!"

She animatedly told him the whole story about how she discovered she was adopted, how she'd found the note her birth mother wrote that her parents never shared with her.

"What an incredible story! Did I ever mention Faith was adopted, too? She found out when she was a little girl and was devastated. She said she'd thought she would never get over her *own* mother not wanting her. Kate tried explaining that her birth mother was just a teenager, that she'd desperately wanted to keep her and raise her on her own, but knew the selfless thing to do was give her up for a better life. Faith wasn't buying it, insisting she just wasn't wanted. I remember Faith telling me she took comfort in the fact that at least there was no such thing as an unwanted *adopted* child."

"Did her birth mother ever try and reach out to her?"

"Not that I know of. It wasn't a secret that she and her brothers were all adopted, but the subject only came up again after we had Ella. She couldn't imagine giving Ella up for *any* reason."

"I'm waiting until after Christmas to write to my birth mother. I hope she still wants to meet me. In her letter she said she wanted to someday, but that was before she got married and had more babies. But I really hope she does. I want to find out who my real father is too, and I think she's the only person who can tell me."

Matt shared things about himself too. He told her how desperate Faith had been to have a baby. How she'd expected to get pregnant on their honeymoon.

Grace mentally did the math and her heart hurt for Faith. Almost three years was a long time to be disappointed each and every month. *All that time and when she finally did get pregnant, she only had those three short months with her baby—so unbearably sad.*

Hearing about them *trying* to have a baby made Grace uncomfortable. It made her wonder what it would be like to be held by him, *loved* by him.

She would be mortified if he could read her thoughts and she steered the conversation onto a less intimate subject.

17

The unusually warm late fall turned into a snowy December. Christmas was right around the corner and Grace was going home to spend it with her parents.

Sadly, she wasn't looking forward to it. She wished she could stay in Eastbrook and watch Ella open her presents on Christmas morning. She wanted to share in the excitement of Mark and Molly opening theirs, too. But she'd never spent a Christmas away from her parents, and she knew they'd be devastated.

Of course, as always, her parents were thrilled to have her home. They made over her so much she almost felt like an idol.

They wanted to know all about her life in Eastbrook. They hung on her every word. Grace couldn't stop talking about Ella and what a special little girl she was.

"It sounds like you've fallen in love with little Ella," her mom commented after Grace told a particularly poignant story.

"I have. I can't imagine her not being a part of my life. I wish I could freeze time."

"And you get along with her father fine?"

"He's wonderful. We've actually developed a nice friendship."

"Do you think you could ever become more than just "friends'"?

"Not really. I don't think he'll ever get over his first wife. They really had something special."

"But he's so young. I can't imagine he'd want to remain a single dad the rest of his life."

Grace didn't want to talk about it. Of course, *she* would love to be more than just friends, but Matt never indicated he saw her as anything more than a friend and Ella's nanny.

She changed the subject. "I can't wait for you to come see my little house. Mother, you'll love it. It's perfect for me; maybe you can come visit when the weather gets nicer. Help me choose what to plant and where to plant them, so that maybe I can make my own little yard look as glorious as yours always does."

"I would love to come help you. What a beautiful answer to prayer that house was! Your father and I are so happy for you, Grace. You seem happier and and more carefree than we've ever seen you. Being a nanny suits you, but do you ever miss your old job?

"A little. I don't miss the people much or living in the city, but I miss the work itself. I know I was good at it. It was rewarding."

"Maybe you could do some freelance work from home. Keep your foot in the door."

Grace remembered Annie making the same suggestion when she first considered the idea of being a nanny. It was a good idea. After all, her job didn't require an office.

Her parents always hated to see her leave, their life revolved around her, but it was the first time in a long time that they didn't feel like they had to worry about her. She seemed happy and they could feel her excitement about moving into her own place.

They insisted on accompanying her right to her gate at the airport. *Really, you would think she was twelve years old.* When it was time to board, they huddled briefly to pray. They stayed and watched the airplane pull away, waving just in case she was seated at a window seat and could see them.

Tears filled Jean's eyes. "Our baby girl is all grown up."

"And she's happy," Bill added. When he noticed the tears in Jean's eyes, he pulled her into an embrace. "You've been a good mother to her, Jean. She is who she is because of you."

"I couldn't bring myself to ask her if she'd tried to contact her real mom."

"I think she'll tell us if or when she does. And remember what she said, Jean. She said she'd never consider anyone but *you* as her 'real' mom."

Grace was eager to get back to Eastbrook. She was biting at the bit to move into her little house. A missionary couple at Annie's church had been home on furlough, but they were returning to the field right after Christmas. They wouldn't be back for another four years. They'd left the house sparsely furnished and told her she was free to add anything and decorate it anyway she chose.

It was just a little bungalow, but compared to the tiny apartment she'd lived in in New York, it was a veritable mansion.

She threw herself into decorating. She painted the walls, bought a few throw pillows and an over stuffed chair and an ottoman. She bought colorful throws to warm up the plain sofa. She found a beautiful hand-made quilt for her bed. In just a few weeks, she'd turned it into a warm and cozy home she was proud to call her own.

She still spent plenty of evenings with Annie and her family, but she loved coming home to her own place, sleeping in her own bed.

Having her own place gave her much more time to herself and she thought of her mother's suggestion of possibly doing some editing from home. On a whim she contacted her old boss to see if he thought it'd be feasible. To Grace's surprise and delight, he responded quickly and welcomed her idea, willing to give her as many jobs as she thought she could handle.

The timing couldn't have been more perfect and she jumped at the chance. Her editing work filled her evenings and kept her busy on the weekends.

Before she knew it, spring would be arriving and she could begin working on making the outside of her home just as colorful and beautiful as the inside.

18

It didn't take Grace long to track down her birth mother. Just like her mother said, she hadn't moved from the small Kentucky town Grace was born in.

Grace wrote a simple letter, saying little more than she'd just recently discovered she was adopted and would like to meet her. If Janet chose not to, she would understand and respect her wishes.

Almost a month went by without hearing from Janet. She tried not to be too disappointed. She'd known there was a very real possibility Janet wouldn't want to disrupt what sounded like a perfect life. If Grace had remained a secret all these years, it would be especially difficult.

Janet's heart lurched when she saw the name on the return address. Grace Ryan. Her Grace was finally reaching out to her!

Janet hadn't seen any reason to tell anyone about Grace because she knew there was a very real possibility Grace would never want to have anything to do with her.

A fresh wave of shame washed over her at the thought of admitting to all her friends and her children that she'd had an out of wedlock baby and given her up for adoption.

It was pride that didn't want her secret paraded out for all the world to see. Pride that didn't want her children to learn something about her that might bring her off the pedestal they may have put her on. And yet. It *was* a part of her story, it had made her *who* she was. She knew even if she *could* un-do it, she wouldn't.

Thank goodness she didn't have any secrets from Jack. Her precious Jack who had himself delivered her first little girl just a little over twenty-five years ago. What a rock he'd been! It'd taken months for him to convince Janet she deserved to be loved by someone like him. Months to talk her into letting him take her out on a real date.

He claimed he fell in love with her at first sight, as soon as he walked into the hospital room and watched her bravely trying to endure the pain of childbirth all by herself. It was their private joke that she fell in love with him as soon as he administered the anesthetic that took that pain away.

God had been good and blessed them with four healthy, happy children. Their love for each other grew through the years and she knew their marriage was stronger than ever—so strong she hardly ever thought of Brett anymore.

After Janet gave birth to Grace, she stayed on at The Haven. Eva needed the help and it was rewarding work. Because she'd walked in their shoes, she was able to give words of comfort and encouragement to the girls who found themselves there.

But when abortion became legal and it became more and more acceptable to give birth out of wedlock, the need for a place like The Haven diminished. Eva eventually sold it to a couple who ended up turning it into a Bed and Breakfast. Eva bought a home near Jack and Janet and continued to do volunteer work at the hospital. Eva was like a second mom to Janet and a doting "grandmother" to their children.

Yes, her life was full and happy. She wouldn't change a thing. She knew she'd be judged by many, and her children might think less of her or be resentful she'd kept a sibling a secret. But the pain and shame would be nothing compared to how awful she'd feel if she chose *not* to acknowledge Grace. Her prayers were finally being answered and her first baby was at long last reaching out to her.

When Janet showed the letter to Jack, he thought of his own secret. He knew if Janet had known she'd delivered twins she would have, at the very least, insisted the girls stay together. What would Janet do if *both* daughters reached out to her? But all these years had passed without a word from either of them and so he'd been able to push his own role in the deception out of his mind.

Janet didn't want to reply to Grace's letter until she'd told the kids about the sister they never knew about. Jack insisted on being with her when she told them.

They took it much better than she'd thought they would. She'd been afraid of losing their respect. Afraid of the questions they might ask about Brett. Questions about *how* it could have happened. But, it was another era and, thank God, they only seemed interested in Grace.

It took Janet dozens of sheets of paper before she was satisfied with the letter.

My dear Grace,

So many years have passed that I'd given up hope of ever meeting you and explaining face to face that I loved you too much to keep you. Every year on your birthday, I remember the joy that surged through me when they held you up for me to see—a beautiful, healthy baby girl.

I have kept my promise to pray for you daily.

When I received your letter I was overcome with joyful trepidation. My decision to give you up has remained a well kept secret, but I love you no

> *less than your brothers and sisters. I've waited to write because I wanted the chance to tell my story,* ***our*** *story, to my friends and family.*
>
> *From the postmark, I see that we live several hundred miles from each other. However, I am very eager to meet you. Would you be willing to meet me half way? I have a very flexible schedule and can accommodate whatever day you choose.*

Janet didn't know how to sign it. She certainly couldn't sign it Mother or Mom. After all, she hadn't been a mother to Grace. Someone else had filled that role. She finally settled on a simple "*Love, Janet.*"

She enclosed a family picture with her phone number written on the back.

19

After weeks of eagerly sifting through her mail in hopes of a reply from her birth mother, when it finally came Grace tore it open and read it and re-read it several times, and then studied the photo. She was shocked how young and lovely Janet was—she looked more like her sister than her mother.

Though Grace was thrilled Janet was open to meeting her, she was disappointed there wasn't any mention of her birth father. Grace wondered if the omission was to protect her. Was he a criminal? Had Janet been raped? Regardless of who he was or what he'd done, Grace was determined to find him, too.

It took Grace a few days to work up the nerve to call her. A child answered the phone and when she asked to speak to Janet, dropped the phone without answering, yelling out, "Mom! Phone!"

When Janet said hello, Grace was silent for a minute, and in that brief moment of silence, Janet knew it was Grace.

They made plans to meet the following week.

Grace arrived at the restaurant first, sat in a booth where she could watch the door. She recognized Janet immediately and waved her over. Janet was dressed in tasteful black pants and a soft blue cashmere sweater set that set off her blue eyes.

She was even more beautiful in person. She approached Grace and smiled warmly. Her big smile revealed a deep dimple in her right cheek.

Janet was momentarily dumbstruck when she got close enough to see Grace's eyes. They were *exactly* like Brett's. She would have recognized her anywhere. The same big, beautiful clear green eyes framed by those beautiful eyelashes. Her breath caught in her throat, remembering how those eyes could melt her heart. Grace stood up and they hugged awkwardly.

After their initial nervousness, they slipped into easy conversation. Janet told Grace about her half siblings, told her they all were eager to meet her. She told her briefly about Jack, how they'd met and eventually married. A typical "patient falling in love with her doctor" story.

"Just think," Janet said with a catch in her voice, "if it hadn't been for you, I would never have met Jack, and I can't imagine my life without him."

Janet wanted to know every detail about Grace's life. Grace was surprised how freely she talked about her upbringing, her friend Annie, college, her job in New York, how her heart had been broken and about the perfect timing of the nanny position.

She told her about Ella, how she'd grown to love her like her own child.

"But in spite of your prayers for me, Janet, I've made some bad choices. My parents don't know about my missteps, it would break their hearts. I think I may have messed up too much to be given the husband you've prayed I'd find."

Janet impulsively reached across the table and grabbed Grace's hand. "There is no such thing as messing up too much. That's why I wanted to name you Grace. It's all about God's grace and mercy. 'His mercies are new every morning,' I know you've been taught that."

Grace gave her a half smile, "You sound just like Annie."

"Look at my life, Grace. I was seventeen years old, unmarried and pregnant. Don't you think I felt the same way you do? But God brought good out of my mistake. It's such a waste of time and energy looking back, longing for a redo. We're never gonna *stop* making mistakes—but God can use them to humble us and give us more empathy for others' missteps. You could never do *anything* to make God love you any less, so don't be so hard on yourself."

Grace's eyes filled with tears. "I was always told 'you can make your choices, but can't choose your consequences'. That's where I'm at right now, paying the consequences of the bad choices I've made."

Janet sadly shook her head in disagreement.

Grace sighed resignedly, before continuing, "Anyway, you were practically a little girl when you made your *one* little mistake. It probably wasn't even your fault. You were too innocent to know better. He took advantage of you. I was older, my sins were willful. I knew exactly what I was doing and I did it anyway."

"I wish that were so, Grace. I *did* know what I was doing, and I probably would have kept on doing it had your father not been so adamant about not letting it happen again."

Grace inhaled deeply before saying, "That's the first time you've mentioned my father. Can you tell me about him? Why *he* didn't want me?"

In all the years Janet prayed Grace would find her, she never considered Grace might want to find her father, too. All these years later the picture of Marilyn in Brett's arms still had the power to hurt her. It was painful to relive the memories, but Grace deserved to know the story.

"His name is Brett Collins and he never even knew I was pregnant."

"How could that be? How did you keep it from him?"

Janet slowly shared the story. As she told it, Grace could see glimpses of the young love they'd shared. Janet said Brett grew up poor, in an unhappy, unloving home.

"His father was a Methodist minister of a small church. Brett never talked about his home life, but I knew his father was a mean man. There were rumors he'd 'taken up' with several women in his congregation. Brett hated 'religion,' as he called it and I expect his father was part of the reason. He wanted out of that little town in the worst way."

Janet sighed, remembering, "We often talked about where we would live, about his dreams of going to college and becoming a doctor. He was over the moon when the University of Michigan offered him a scholarship that paid for everything. When I found out I was pregnant, I knew Brett would insist on doing the right thing and marrying me. That would mean giving up his scholarship and I couldn't bear the thought of making him give up that dream." Janet's eyes filled with tears. *Wow,* Grace thought, *she really* ***had*** *loved him.*

Janet drew in a deep breath before continuing, "He was planning on leaving for school the first week in September, I figured I was due with you right around the first of the New Year. It was early August and I still wasn't showing. Right before he came home for his Christmas break I planned on telling him I needed to go spend some time with a sick relative, but I'd be back before he had to leave for school. Of course, I wouldn't make it back, but I'd be home before he came home for his Easter break. I figured I would have had you by then, that you'd be placed in a family who would love you and raise you to know and love Jesus and that no one would ever have to know about it."

Janet looked wistful, "But looking back, I know I couldn't have gone through with it. I couldn't have given you up or kept that secret from him. But at the time, all I knew was that I loved him too much to take away his dream of going to college."

Janet told her about Brett's first girlfriend, Marilyn. How insecure she'd made Janet feel. She said she'd always worried he'd go back to her. "So I don't know why I was so shocked when I saw them in each other's arms that day." Just telling the story made the pain seem real again.

Janet sighed before continuing, "The day after I saw them in the dime store, my parents and I went to visit The Haven and I never left. Eva, the woman who ran the home, became a second mother to me. I caught her passion to match unplanned, undesired babies up with loving

Christian parents. I loved those poor girls who came to live with us until their babies were born.

After I married Jack, we didn't waste any time having babies of our own. Your younger sister, Beth, is only twenty-three, just two years younger than you. Amy is twenty-one, John is fifteen and our little surprise baby, Bobby, just turned five. I've enjoyed every minute of being a wife and mother. Honestly, I wouldn't change a thing."

"I'm happy for you Janet. I think I would have done the same thing."

Grace haltingly told her the story of the night she'd been raped. "I've thought about how awful it would have been if I'd gotten pregnant with Philip's baby." Grace shuddered at the thought. "I could never have had an abortion, but I can see myself giving that baby to a family that desperately wanted one."

Even after all these years, the memory of that night with Phillip filled her with nervous tension and debilitating guilt. She wanted to change the subject.

"Guess how I found out about you? It's the best part."

She told Janet how bereft and heartbroken she'd felt when she left New York, how desperate she was to feel close to God again.

She told how she'd laid on her childhood bed and begged God to show her He was real. She told her how she pulled that old Bible off the shelf and Janet's prayer fell out of it.

Grace pulled out her wallet and carefully removed the yellowed piece of notepaper and passed it over to Janet. Janet's hands shook as she read it, she gulped back a sob, remembering the heartache of giving up her baby. "My prayers haven't *all* been answered. I'll be praying God will bring that husband along soon."

"I think I may have nullified the contract when I didn't keep the 'temple' pure and sweet."

"That's a lie, Grace. Don't you dare believe the lies the evil one tries to feed us. Look at my life. I never dreamed I'd have a life this full, with a husband who adores me and four healthy children. I fall deeper in love with Jack each passing year. I can't conceive of my life without him. God made all that happen, Grace. It sure wasn't because I remained a pure vessel."

Grace sat unconvinced.

"Do you have a boyfriend? Someone you're interested in?"

Grace looked down at her hands, "There *is* someone I'm interested in," she said softly before looking up. "But he isn't available."

"Who is it?"

"Ella's father."

"Why *isn't* he available? Is he dating someone?"

"No. He's just never going to get over Ella's mom. She was so breathtakingly beautiful. Actually other than her red hair, she kind of reminds me of you. She had big blue eyes like yours, and a dimple when she smiled. I think she spoiled him for any other woman. I know I'd never be good enough for him. But, Oh. My. Goodness. He has it all . . . looks, charm, brains . . ."

"Don't sell yourself short, Grace. You have it all, too. You're beautiful, smart, sweet. I am so thankful you found me." Janet looked down at her watch, surprised how quickly the time had gone. "I'm sorry, but I need to get going." They stood up together. Grace impulsively embraced her. Tears filled both their eyes and they held each other for several long seconds.

Finally Grace stepped back, "Thank you, Janet. Thank you for writing that prayer, and praying for me all these years. Thank you for letting me unload with you like I never could with my own parents."

Janet took hold of both of Grace's hands, "I'm not going to stop praying for you, you know that don't you? I'm confident God will continue to answer my prayers, too."

Grace squeezed her hands back in a silent "thank you."

Grace walked Janet to her car. Janet stopped before getting in, she couldn't keep herself from asking, "Are you planning on trying to find Brett?"

"Yes. And when I do, I'll tell you all about him. Who knows? I might even have more half siblings I never knew about."

Janet's heart lurched thinking about what Brett's reaction would be to the secret she'd kept from him. She had hoped she'd never have to face him.

"Oh, no. I don't need to know all about him. I don't *want* to know all about him. I'm sure he's a doctor now, most likely happily married to Marilyn."

"But it's kind of a big deal, you know. Never telling him he fathered a baby. He might not be as understanding as you think."

"Well, he better be! I did him a favor." Janet responded defensively, with a little sharpness to her tone.

"But you didn't let *him* have a say about whether or not *he* wanted to be a part of my life."

Grace could tell Janet was uncomfortable with the turn the conversation had taken. Her face was flushed and her anxiety was palpable. Her voice had a wobble in it, "Well, I hope he'll just let bygones be bygones and understand."

Grace felt sorry for her, "I'm sure he will. I'm sorry. I don't want you worrying about it. But you do understand why I want to find him, don't you? Wouldn't you if you were me?"

Janet bit her bottom lip in consternation, and without answering the question, gave Grace one more quick hug before getting in her car.

Grace drove home feeling happier than she'd felt in months. She couldn't wait to share with Matt how wonderful it'd been to meet her birth mother and learn the story behind her adoption.

She prayed she'd be able to find Brett and that he'd be open to meeting her, too.

She turned up the radio and sang along to the songs, her heart full with possibilities.

20

It took Brett years before he gave up hope of reconnecting with Janet. When things started getting serious with Patty, he felt obligated to make one last ditch effort to find her, if only to assure himself he was really over her.

He'd contacted Janet's parents and asked if he could stop by for a visit and they'd been surprisingly gracious.

Seeing and talking to them brought back those long ago longings, almost convincing him he wasn't ready for marriage after all. But when he learned Janet was happily married and expecting her second child, he knew he had no choice but to move on.

He and Patty were married in less than a year.

~ ~

Brett's first semester in college was a rough one. He had been so sure he and Janet were going to spend the rest of their lives together. When she dropped out of his life without a trace, it left a hole in his heart he didn't think anything could ever fill.

Fortunately, he and his roommate Paul hit it off from the first day. The only thing about Paul that rubbed Brett the wrong way was his faith.

He wasn't buying into it. He'd seen too many supposed "Christians" who treated people like dogs. Brett used to think Janet was the only Christian he knew with a genuinely sweet spirit, one that truly wanted to live her life according to the "scriptures," as she always called it. But she'd turned out to be a phony, too. How could a loving person do to Brett what she'd done?

And then there was his dad. Quoting the Bible even as he whipped Brett bloody almost every day of his young life. He still had scars on his backside from his dad's unwillingness to "spare the rod."

His dad had been a very handsome, charismatic man and Brett knew many of the women in his congregation who sought counseling from him got *a lot* more than just comforting words and supposedly sage advice. He knew his mom knew it too, but she never confronted his dad. She lived with the humiliation. Her resentment grew with each new revelation. She became a bitter woman. Brett never knew what a happy home looked like.

As much as Brett enjoyed his roommate's company, he never hung out with him socially. Brett ran with a wilder crowd. He kept his grades up just enough to keep his scholarship. He got drunk every weekend, and slept with more than a few girls. He regretted every one of them. They only made him miss Janet more. Made him feel guilty for giving them false hope that they meant anything more to him than a single night's pleasure.

As the school year continued, Paul began to give him an entirely different picture of what it meant to be a Christian. Paul never tried to push his faith on Brett, but when they left for summer break he gave him a copy of C.S. Lewis's *Mere Christianity* and asked him if he'd read it. Brett promised he would. And it changed his life.

Brett reluctantly admitted the veracity of Lewis's assertion that Jesus could only be a liar, a lunatic or Lord. It ultimately didn't matter how Christians or supposed Christians acted, it only mattered *who* Jesus was and *what* He had done for a world full of sinners, just like himself. He could no longer deny Jesus as *his* Lord and Savior and he could no longer live his life as if it was his own.

The hole in his heart was finally being filled. When he returned to school, the wild parties no longer interested him and he regretted how disrespectfully he'd treated girls.

He would never forget the night he admitted to Paul the impact Lewis's book had made. How it convinced him to accept Jesus as Lord. They knelt together beside Brett's bed, and tears slipped down Brett's cheeks as he listened to Paul's prayer of thanksgiving for a new brother in Christ.

Brett began accompanying Paul to a campus Bible study and that's where he met Patty. She was a natural beauty, rarely wore make-up and usually wore her long, dark hair pulled back in a ponytail. She had the biggest heart of anyone he'd ever met. He hadn't been immediately attracted to her, but they became good friends and in time she became more to him than just a friend. He began to see her as the person he wanted to spend his life with, to have babies with and grow old with.

He remembered the night he asked her to marry him, how he'd whispered he could hardly wait to start a family.

She'd pulled back, tears in her eyes. "I should have told you sooner. But, I loved you from the beginning and I was afraid you would never want to be more than friends if you knew."

Brett reassuringly rubbed her back, waiting for her to continue.

"I was born with only one ovary." She was looking away when she said it, she didn't want to see the disappointment in his eyes.

"So? That doesn't mean you can't get pregnant and have a perfectly normal pregnancy."

"But it might mean I'll have a harder time getting pregnant. What if it never happens?"

Brett couldn't pretend it wasn't a big deal to him. He'd always wanted to be a dad.

"We'll deal with that if or when it happens." He pulled her close and kissed the top of her head. "I love you, Patty. Through thick or thin, you're my gal."

But as each year went by without a pregnancy, Brett's dream of being a father died a slow death—until Grace called him out of the blue and claimed to be his daughter.

He and Patty were snuggling on the couch, munching on a bowl of popcorn and watching an old movie. When the phone rang, Patty pressed pause on the VCR and slipped into the kitchen to answer it.

"Hello?"

"May I speak to Brett Collins, please?"

"May I ask what it's concerning?" Patty normally didn't probe, because more often than not it was one of Brett's patients calling for one reason or another. But the woman on the other line called him Brett, not Doctor.

"Uh. It's kind of personal. Maybe I can call back at a better time? Or give you my number and he can call me when it's convenient?"

"He's here. Hold on a minute please."

"Brett?" Patty called him into the kitchen. When he came in, she handed him the phone. Out of curiosity, she stayed to listen.

"Hello."

Grace's heart raced when she heard the deep voice that was, in all probability, her father's. She'd practiced what she was going to say, but when she heard his voice, her well thought out words left her.

"Hello?" Brett repeated.

"Er. Yes. Hello. I was kind of surprised how easy it was to find you . . ."

"To find me? Find me for what?"

"To let you know you have a daughter you never knew about." *Shucks! Those weren't the words she'd practiced.*

Brett thought frantically back to his first year at Michigan. *Had one of the girls he'd casually slept with hid a pregnancy from him all these years?*

"Do you remember dating a Janet Roberts in high school?"

"Of course." *How could he ever forget his first love?*

"Well, anyway, I just recently discovered I was adopted and that Janet was my birth mother, and so I wrote her a letter and she finally wrote me back, and we agreed to meet and . . ."

Brett remained silent as Grace prattled on ". . . she told me the only reason she never told you about me was because she didn't want you to give up your dream of college."

"She had no right," he responded tersely.

"I might agree with you, but I'd rather talk in person, I have something to show you . . . if you want to meet me, that is. We actually only live about forty minutes from each other and . . ."

He didn't even allow her to finish her sentence, "Of course I want to meet you! Just tell me where and when."

They arranged to meet at the diner in downtown Eastbrook.

Patty watched Brett closely as he talked. She saw how his shoulders tensed, watched his jaw tighten in consternation. Whomever and whatever the woman on the other line was saying was having a powerful effect on his demeanor. And *now* he was agreeing to meet her somewhere? Patty had never felt a smidgeon of jealousy. Despite all the beautiful nurses always vying for his attention, she never questioned his devotion to her. But he wasn't even acknowledging her presence beside him as he spoke, and for the first time she felt a touch of insecurity.

After their conversation, Brett hung up the phone and put his head in his hands. *The* ***one*** *time he and Janet went too far resulted in a pregnancy she never told him about? How could she have doubted he would have made it work, that he would have done anything for her?*

"Honey? What's wrong? Who was that?" Patty pressed, interrupting his reverie.

How was he going to explain this to Patty? He'd never told her about Janet. What would he have told her? That his heart had been broken so badly when he was a teenager he'd thought he might lose his mind?

No, he had kept Janet in a private corner of his mind, rarely allowing himself to revisit the sweet memories. Now, one phone call brought them all back.

"You aren't going to believe it . . ."

He slowly told her about Janet. They were so young. It was so long ago.

His memories of the day at the lake were as sharp as ever but he made as light of it as he could, "It was just that *one* time . . ."

Patty felt a simmering resentment. She could tell by Brett's voice that he had truly loved this girl from his youth. ***Why** God? Why was life so unfair? I've been so desperate to make Brett a father, and yet You let some teenager he was with **one** time get pregnant and then just let her give his baby away? **Why**?*

"It *is* hard to believe, Brett. *Do* you believe it?" Patty tried to keep the resentment out of her voice.

"Only because I don't think Janet would lie about it. She, her name is Grace, said she only found out she was adopted last fall. She found Janet, and Janet told her I was her father."

"And now she wants to meet you?"

Brett nodded, stood up and pulled Patty into his arms.

21

When Brett walked into the diner, Grace's back was to him. His heart leapt in his chest because he thought it *was* Janet. Her hair was exactly the same, she had on a form-fitting sweater that showed off her beautiful shoulders that were so much like Janet's.

But then she turned and looked at him with *his* same eyes. It was uncanny.

She gave him a knowing grin. "I guess there's no doubt, is there?"

"None at all." He smiled and Grace could instantly see why Janet had been so smitten with him.

He slipped into the opposite booth, eager to hear everything she had to tell him.

Grace poured out the whole story, how she'd found the prayer.

"In fact, I have it with me. It's what I wanted you to show you." She reached into her purse and took out the faded piece of notepaper and handed it to him.

Reading it, written so carefully in Janet's neat cursive, caused long buried emotions to surface once again. It was hard to imagine she'd only been seventeen when she'd written it.

He wanted to feel nothing but anger for what Janet had done, yet he couldn't help but feel sympathy for the scared, brave girl she must have been. He felt that old twinge of guilt for stealing her innocence, for not having more control that day. *But who would have believed that* ***one*** *time,* ***one*** *time, for crying out loud, could have resulted in this . . . this beautiful woman in front of him?*

When he finished reading it, he swallowed the lump in his throat and handed it back to Grace, "I don't know what to say. I don't know how she could have left me out on her decision. I loved her with everything I had, she *had* to know I wouldn't have let her handle it on her own . . ."

"She said she did you a favor . . ."

"Well, she didn't," Brett responded a little more hotly than he intended. "She robbed me of the chance of knowing you, of being your father, of . . ." *But what good did it do to be angry* ***now****? The hands of time couldn't be turned back.* He took a steadying breath and forced a smile. "But there's nothing we can do about it now, can we? We can only start from now."

Brett wanted to know everything about her. Several hours passed in a flash.

Brett walked her out to her car, stopping her just before she got in, "Thank you, Grace. Thank you for looking me up. I hope you know I'm determined to try and make up for all the years I've missed out on. I can't wait for you to meet Patty. You're gonna love her."

"I'm sure I will. And thank *you* for meeting me. Like I told you, God led me to that prayer, and then to Janet and now to you. And I can't help but believe *you* are part of the reason God brought me here to Eastbrook."

Brett hadn't looked at it that way. Grace had a point. If things hadn't unfolded the way they did, she might never have stumbled upon the prayer, and he might never had learned he'd fathered a child. God did indeed work in mysterious ways.

In a few short months, Grace became a fixture in Brett and Patty's lives. Grace fell in love with Patty, just as Brett knew she would.

They loved hearing her stories about Ella. They could tell Grace loved her like her own.

"You need to bring her with you the next time you come out, we'd love to meet the little lady."

Grace agreed, bringing Ella with her on her very next visit. Of course Ella charmed their socks off. Just like everyone else they met, they were astounded at the similarity of their eyes. Brett, Grace and Ella *all* blessed with those unusually, clear green eyes.

Brett and Patty began spoiling Ella with toys and clothes and Brett promised to build her a playhouse just as soon as the weather got nicer.

It made Grace happy knowing she'd brought a new fullness to Brett and Patty's life. They'd not only gained a daughter, but it was as though they'd gained a granddaughter as well.

22

As the months went by, Matt struggled to identify his feelings for Grace. He knew he wanted to be with her as much as possible, thought of everything under the sun to keep her talking and lingering each night.

He wished for time alone with her without Ella constantly interrupting. He thought how nice it would be to take her out for dinner, have her all to himself. And why *shouldn't* he ask her out? It wasn't as if she had anyone else in her life. The only other people she ever talked about were Brett and Patty, her friend Annie and her husband and kids.

He could tell by the way she held and kissed Ella she genuinely cared for her. But what if it didn't go so well? Would he lose her as a nanny? He knew he'd never be able to replace her—and Ella would be devastated.

But, then again, what if it *did* work? How many times had Matt daydreamed about her being his wife? He'd been sure when Faith died he'd never marry again, he couldn't even imagine being attracted to another woman. But he couldn't deny his growing attraction to Grace.

Annie and Jimmy had several single friends they were constantly trying to fix Grace up with. They invited a bunch of them over one night to play games and Grace agreed to go. She had fun but couldn't see herself dating any of the guys. She couldn't help but compare them to Matt, and of course, they all fell way short.

She could tell one of the guys was particularly into her. He took pains to sit next to her and engage her in conversation. He was nice enough, halfway decent looking, laughed easily. Why couldn't she be attracted to him?

He waited until Grace was ready to leave and followed her out to her car. He touched her shoulder as she opened her car door.

"Hey. I was wondering if you might be free Friday night? *Grease* is showing at the Cinema Plex. I thought we could go to dinner first and then go see the movie."

Grace was caught off guard and couldn't think of a legitimate reason to say no.

"Uh, sure." She agreed without any enthusiasm.

"Great! I'll pick you up at seven?"

"Sure. See you then."

Grace berated herself for not having the backbone to tell this guy she wasn't interested. But would it really be that bad? Could she just be flattered someone was interested in her and enjoy some male company for once?

The thing was, she *was* enjoying some male company. But Matt wasn't available, would never be available. She needed to quit comparing him to every guy she met.

Matt finally convinced himself to ask Grace out. He made reservations for Friday night at the country club; they could sit outside, enjoy a chilled bottle of wine and watch the sunset. Though Matt enjoyed his membership for the golfing, he never stayed over with the guys for drinks. But it was a beautiful place and the food was great.

He waited until midweek to tell her about his plans. He was actually feeling a little nervous. It had been a long time since he'd asked a girl out. Plus, he was acutely aware of how dating would change the dynamics of their relationship.

He pleaded with Grace that night to stay and eat with them and Grace agreed. He wouldn't let her clear the table, suggested instead they take Ella out to the backyard and let her play in her sandbox. He brought two lawn chairs out of the garage for them to sit on.

Neither of them spoke for a few minutes, happy to sit silently and watch Ella make sand castles.

Finally, Matt looked at her, admiring her perfect profile, the contented half smile on her face.

"Grace?"

Grace turned to him, waiting for him to continue. The way the sunlight touched her skin and made her clear green eyes appear brighter made him catch his breath. A tendril of hair had come loose from her ponytail, she tucked the spiral behind one ear and raised an inquisitive eyebrow.

"I made dinner reservations at the club for Friday night."

"Did you want me to stay with Ella?

"No, I already asked Kate if she would watch her. I was thinking maybe you and I could go. Thought it might be nice to talk without Ella constantly interrupting us."

Grace's heart sunk. ***Why** had she ever agreed to go out with that dweeb friend of Annie's?*

Grace's hesitation convinced Matt she wasn't interested. He was taken aback by how deeply disappointed he was.

"I wish I could . . ." *I really, really, really wish I could.* "But I made plans to, uh, go see a movie."

Matt tried not to ask, but couldn't help himself, "With Annie?"

"No, with some guy that was at one of their parties last weekend."

"Oh. Well. Good for you." He smiled stiffly and kicked himself for assuming she'd be free and would want to go out with him. For assuming there weren't any other guys in her life. He was embarrassed he'd been confident enough to make a reservation that he'd now have to cancel.

Grace wanted to explain she had no desire to go out with this guy, but had been caught off guard and couldn't come up with a reason to say no, but Matt stood up before she could say anything.

"I guess I should probably take Ella in and get her in the bathtub. Thanks again for dinner. I'll see you in the morning."

"Sure." Grace wanted to add more, but he strode over to the sandbox without looking back.

Grace called Annie as soon as she walked in the door. "I could kick myself for not having enough backbone to tell that dweeb friend of yours that I wasn't interested."

"Wow. That sounds a bit harsh. Poor David. What did he do to bring on such an angry onslaught?"

"Matt asked me out. For *Friday night.*"

"Oh . . ."

"Can you believe it?? For the first time in forever I have plans and Matt asks me to go out on *that* night."

"Grace, calm down. He's obviously interested, he'll ask again."

"He might not. He was very abrupt with me after I told him I had plans."

"Of course he was! He was disappointed. He'll come around."

"I'm afraid it will change everything. We've gotten comfortable with each other, talking and laughing like regular friends. I don't want to lose that."

"I'm sure he doesn't either. He certainly doesn't want to lose *you.*"

Grace had to admit there was truth in that statement. She had managed to make herself invaluable. Maybe he would ask her out again, but regardless she had to force herself to regard him as nothing more than a friend and an employer. *Yeah, right.*

When Grace arrived at the house the next morning, there was definitely a tension that wasn't there before. Matt was terse with her, not exchanging any of the usual pleasantries.

Matt couldn't stop thinking about Grace on his way to work. Why had he let some guy beat him to the punch? What if Grace fell for this dude? He couldn't stand envisioning her with another guy. The guy would undoubtedly fall for Grace. How could any man *not* fall for her? She was smart, funny and beautiful.

If she *did* fall for this guy he would have to force himself to stifle his personal feelings for her because he certainly couldn't afford to lose her as a nanny.

When Matt got home from work on Friday, he couldn't keep himself from mentioning her date that night.

"So tonight's the big date, eh?"

"Not exactly a 'big' date, but yeah, tonight's the night." Grace gave him a weak smile and Matt knew his Friday night would be longer and lonelier than usual.

Grace drove home wishing more than ever she'd been free to accept Matt's offer to dine at the country club.

David arrived right on time. He looked nice in his khakis and crisp white button down shirt. He smelled good, too. He couldn't have been more polite or interested in hearing everything about her. But he wasn't Matt.

She did love the movie. They both did. He put a casual arm behind her seat at the theatre, but thankfully didn't try to hold her hand or press in too close for comfort.

When they arrived back at her home, she thanked him for a nice night and opened her door before he had a chance to answer. He leaped out and walked around to meet her and offer to walk her to her door.

"Oh, no. I'm fine. Really."

"I had a great night with you, Grace. Can we do it again?"

Ugh. Just what I hoped to avoid. "I . . . um. Maybe." *Why can't I just say "no?"*

She stepped away from him, thereby escaping an awkward hug or an attempted good night kiss. She walked deliberately up the sidewalk before turning towards him and giving a friendly wave, "Thanks again!"

When Grace arrived at Matt's Monday morning she was surprised to find him completely dressed, sitting at the kitchen table drinking his coffee and reading the paper.

"I'm not used to seeing this." Grace smiled. "Do you have an early meeting? I could have come earlier."

"Nah. I don't have a meeting. For some reason, I woke up before my alarm and decided I'd get up and get dressed. Not be in a hurry for once. Sit down and have a cup of coffee with me."

Grace had gotten used to her routine. Let herself into the house, pour herself a freshly brewed cup of coffee and wait for Matt to come down. Grace felt Matt's eyes on her as she poured her coffee.

Matt noted Grace had on the same jeans and t-shirt she'd worn the very first day. Oh, how the stirrings of desire he'd felt that day had magnified since getting to know her. When she turned around and found him staring at her, her smile faded, her heart quickened.

Before she even sat down, he spoke, "How was the date?"

Grace was secretly thrilled at his curiosity. "It was fine. Nothing special."

"Did he ask you out for a second date?"

"Yes." She wasn't going to offer up the details, enjoying his inability to contain his curiosity.

"What did you say?"

"I said, 'maybe'."

"Hmmmm." Matt was quiet a moment before standing up and grabbing his sport coat from the back of the chair. "I guess I better get going." He gave her a tight lipped smile. "Have a good day."

As soon as the door closed, Grace felt bereft. The satisfaction his curiosity brought evaporated, leaving in its place disappointment and emptiness. How would he have responded if she'd told him there wasn't a chance she'd ever go out with David again? What if she'd told him she couldn't help wishing all night long she had been with him instead? Her silly pride had kept her from admitting as much.

23

It was a mid-summer day; they were expecting lots of sun and temperatures in the 90's. Grace brought her swimsuit with her to Matt's. She told him she thought it was a perfect day for her and Ella to play in the sprinkler.

While driving into work, Matt couldn't stop thinking about Grace in a swimsuit. Mid-morning, he picked up the phone and called home.

Grace's heart skipped a beat at the sound of his rich baritone. "It's supposed to be a scorcher today."

Grace took a deep breath before answering, "That's what they say." *Surely he hadn't called to discuss the weather?*

"I was thinking maybe you and Ella might want to spend the day at the country club. They have a nice swimming pool. Might be a little more fun than running through the sprinkler. Maybe Annie and her kids would want to go with you."

"That sounds wonderful! But can we just show up? Don't we need to be members or something?"

"Nope. It's enough that I'm a member. I'll call and tell them you're coming. No problem. So you think it's something you want to do?"

"Definitely. I know Ella would love it."

"Great. I'll give them a call then. See ya tonight."

Annie was as thrilled as Grace at the prospect of lounging around the pool for the day. She promised to pack up the kids and pick up Ella and Grace within minutes.

Just as Matt promised, Grace gave the security guard their names and they welcomed them right in.

Grace and Annie were enjoying themselves almost as much as the kids. They sat at the edge of the pool with their legs dangling in the water, laughing and visiting as they watched the kids squeal with pleasure as they played in the water. The time passed quickly and as much as they hated to leave, they knew they needed to start packing up to head home.

"Ten more minutes," Grace suggested. "I'll jump in one more time and as soon as I'm dry we'll pack up."

~ ~

Matt couldn't concentrate at work, he kept picturing Grace in her bathing suit, swimming and playing with Ella. Maybe he'd take the rest of the day off, he was useless anyway. He could drive back home, grab his suit and head up to the club and surprise them.

~ ~

Just as Grace emerged from the water and pulled herself back up onto the pool ledge, she spotted Matt striding out of the men's locker room, his eyes scanning the crowded pool looking for them. Grace's breath caught in her throat as she gaped blatantly at his bare broad shoulders and narrow hips.

She wondered if Matt was aware of the admiring glances he was getting from the women. He stood directly across the pool from her, and when his eyes finally landed on her, he took her in much the same way she'd gawked at him.

She felt self-conscious in her skimpy red bikini, almost naked. She'd planned on running through the sprinkler with Ella, not coming to some fancy-schmancy country club.

At the sight of Grace, Matt's heart skipped a beat. She must have spotted him first, because she was staring and smiling at him. Her hair was all slicked back from her face, the water making her skin glisten. The way her wet suit clung to her body left little to the imagination. She looked like a goddess. His body involuntarily responded to the sight of her and he made a neat dive into the pool and came up right in front of her, playfully tugging on her ankles before he surfaced.

Grace looked at the way his black lashes spiked around his eyes, the way his deep brown eyes glanced over her body before meeting her eyes.

"It was such a beautiful day, I decided to take the rest of the day off. Surprise you and . . ."

Before he could finish Ella spotted him, "Daddddeeeee!!"

"Ella-Bella!"

Ella skipped over to the edge of the pool and launched herself at Matt, confident she'd be caught safely in his arms.

Matt swung her around, put her back up on the pool ledge and let her jump to him over and over again.

When Ella finally tired of the game, she pointed at Grace, "Now Momma Gwace. Momma Gwace jump to Daddy."

Matt looked at Grace and winked, "Don't worry Momma Gwace, I can catch you."

Ella started clapping her hands excitedly. "Jump! Jump!"

Grace good-naturedly stood up and jumped neatly into the water, feeling Matt's hands encircling her waist in a pretense of "catching" her.

He didn't immediately remove his hands, the intensity of his gaze and the warmth of his hands on her bare midriff made Grace shyly lower her eyes. There was no denying the pull of attraction simmering between them.

"It's nice to see you, Matt. Thanks for letting us come use your pool," Annie's voice interrupted their mutual enthrallment with each other.

Grace had completely forgotten about Annie! She must have walked away as soon as Matt surfaced. She had Mark and Molly in tow and their belongings all packed up and ready to go.

"Grace, would it be okay if Matt gives you a ride home? These two definitely need a nap." She gave Grace a big grin and a knowing look that said she was doing her a big favor.

Matt jumped out of the water, embarrassed he hadn't acknowledged Annie. He reached out and took her hand, "It's great to see you, Annie. It's been a long time. But Grace talks about you so much I feel like I know you better than I do."

"Your little Ella is beautiful! Mark and Molly have so much fun playing with her and you can't imagine how thrilled I am to have Grace so close."

"I know she's thrilled to be close to you, too. You guys have a special friendship."

As they talked, Grace got out of the pool, knelt to kiss each of the kids and then gave Annie a hug goodbye. She thanked Annie for driving and promised to call her later.

Matt and Grace sat back down on the edge of the pool and laughed as they watched Ella splash around.

"Are you good with staying a while?" Matt asked. "I didn't mean to intrude on your time with Annie.

"I'd love to stay a while, neither of us were ready to leave but the kids needed naps, so we were just packing up."

"How about a couple of frozen cocktails and some burgers before we head out? I can pretend I'm on vacation."

"That sounds lovely. But just the cocktail for me, I packed a lunch for me and Ella."

Matt stood up to place their orders and Grace coaxed Ella into taking a break from the pool. She carried her over to a lounge chair, wrapped her in a towel and held her close on her lap. In minutes, Ella was sleeping, snuggled against Grace's chest.

When Matt came back with the drinks, he stopped a few yards short and admired the view of Grace with Ella. Grace bent her head down and pressed her lips on top of Ella's silky curls. He knew Ella held a special place in Grace's heart, if only he could wrangle a place in it for himself too.

Matt handed Grace her drink and bent to kiss Ella's head where Grace's lips had been seconds before.

Grace took a sip of the drink. "Mm. Thank you. What a perfect day this has been. This is a beautiful place. Do you get to enjoy it much?"

"I golf out here when I can. I have a few buddies I play with every other Saturday. Other than that, no. But you and Ella should come out and enjoy it as much as possible while you still can. Make the most what's left of the summer."

"We might just do that."

"Please do. And Grace?"

Grace looked up at the seriousness of his voice.

"Do you have plans this weekend?"

She smiled, "Nope."

"Would you like to come out here for dinner Friday night?"

"I would love to."

Matt gave her his wide grin. "Then it's a date."

The rest of the afternoon was delightful. While Ella slept Matt told her about some of the families that belonged to the club.

"Kind of a ritzy crowd," Grace commented.

"Most of them are actually pretty down to earth. Once you get to know them, you'll see what I mean."

"Did Faith come out here much?" Grace couldn't resist asking.

"We didn't join the club until she was pregnant with Ella, so she didn't have much of a chance to get out here. We were looking forward to that first summer with . . ." Matt's voice trailed off.

"I'm sorry." Grace wished she hadn't brought Faith up. It put a damper on their conversation. Matt became quiet and pensive.

When Ella woke up, they let her play in the water a bit longer before they began packing up. Matt was quiet driving home. Grace wondered if he was thinking about how sad it was that Faith never got a chance to enjoy a summer with Ella.

As Matt drove to Grace's house, he couldn't help but think about what a perfect day he'd had with Grace.

When he pulled up to her house, he grabbed her hand before she could jump out. "Don't forget we have a date Friday."

He continued to hold her hand as he took in her sun-kissed nose and cheeks, admired the shiny curls that surrounded her face and hung halfway down her back. He was used to seeing her hair in a ponytail, never guessing what gloriously beautiful hair she had. "Can you leave your hair down like this Friday night?"

He continued to hold her hand as he spoke, looking at her hair as if it really was something to behold.

"If you'd like," she almost whispered.

"I'd like," he answered softly, still holding her hand. He didn't want the day to end. He searched her face, his eyes settling on her lips. *Oh, how he wanted to kiss those lips.* He finally released her hand and Grace opened the door and got out.

"Thanks again. It was a perfect day. See you in the morning."

Her phone was ringing when Grace walked into her house. She dropped her stuff in the hall and ran to answer it.

"He's even more gorgeous than I remember!" Annie exclaimed before Grace could even say hello.

Grace gave a slight laugh and sighed in agreement.

"He's into you Grace, I can tell."

"He asked me out again."

"I *knew* he would!"

"Well, he sure took his time about it."

"He probably wanted to make sure you weren't interested in the 'dweeb.'"

"Oh, Annie, I'm really falling hard for him. What if it all goes sour? I don't know if I could continue working for him if it did, yet I can't stand the thought of not being a part of Ella's life."

"Come on, Grace. Don't borrow trouble. Enjoy the moment. If it's meant to be, it won't 'go sour,' and if it isn't, God will work out the details. For now, just enjoy yourself. Be yourself. Believe me, based on how he looked at you today, he's smitten."

"Then why is he still wearing his wedding ring?"

"He probably doesn't even think about it. Come on, Grace. Focus on the present. Have fun. A gorgeous, kind and good man is taking you out. Take it for what it's worth."

24

Grace took extra time getting ready Friday night. She had the perfect little black dress, it showed off her tan, toned arms and shoulders and dipped low in the back. It'd been ages since she'd had an occasion to wear it. She left her tan legs bare and slipped on some black, high-heeled sandals. She left her hair down like he'd asked.

When she opened the door to Matt, he looked her up and down and gave a low appreciative whistle. His face broke into his now familiar grin.

"Shall we go, my lady?" He offered his arm and she tucked her hand in the crux of his elbow.

It was a beautiful warm night; Matt had reserved a table out on the patio overlooking the lush golf course. White lights were wrapped around the trees that bordered the patio.

Several people stopped by their table to say hello and ask to be introduced to his beautiful date, and he proudly obliged.

It secretly pleased Grace he had chosen a place for their first date where they were sure to run into people Matt knew. A kind of public proclamation that he was dating again. But his wedding ring remained on.

Grace couldn't remember a night she enjoyed more. She'd never been on a first date where the conversation flowed as easily. But since they'd become close friends, it really wasn't like a "first" date.

They lingered long after finishing their meal, listening to the band. They started playing one of Grace's favorite love songs and when she told Matt it was one of her favorites, he suggested they dance to it. As they swayed to the music of the familiar song, Grace rested her head on Matt's broad shoulder. Her lips were inches from the hollow of his neck and it took every ounce of will power not to place her lips against his cologne scented skin. *What would he think if she did something that brazen?* She wished the night could last forever.

When the music stopped, Matt continued to hold her close, tipped her chin up and searched her eyes. "Have you had a nice night, Grace?"

"The best. I wish it didn't have to end. Is Kate alright with us staying out this late?"

Matt bent his head down and whispered huskily into her ear, "She took Ella for the night, we can stay out all night long if we like."

Grace felt a rush of nervous excitement. *Had he planned on having an empty house to take Grace home to?* The thought shouldn't excite her, it should appall her, but it didn't.

When the band started packing up their equipment, Matt reluctantly admitted they'd better call it a night.

They held hands as they left the club. He opened the car door for her, and after settling into the driver's seat, he sighed contentedly, "What a night! Thank you, Grace." He grabbed her hand and kissed it gently.

As soon as they pulled out of the driveway, he reached for her hand, held it as they drove. They were quiet on the drive home. Grace wondered if he was considering taking them back to his house. Surely not! Even still, when he turned onto her street she was a little disappointed.

He got out and opened the door for her, taking her hand in his.

They walked up to her door and he let go of her hand while she dug in her purse for her keys.

Grace was so flustered her hands shook as she pulled out her key ring. Matt must have noticed her nervousness because he gently took the keys from her, easily found her house key and unlocked the door for her. He handed her back her keys without opening the door.

He put his hands on her small waist, his eyes taking in her whole face before dropping his gaze to her lips. He lowered his head and placed his lips on hers for a soft, gentle kiss goodnight. "Thank you for a wonderful night, Grace," he whispered against her lips, before lifting his his head and dropping his hands from her waist. He walking away before Grace had a chance to thank *him*.

Grace stood outside of her door a minute, watched him walk away and tried not to be hurt by the abruptness of his goodbye. When he got in his car without looking back, she finally opened the door. She pressed her back against the closed door and sighed. *Had something gone wrong for the date to end so abruptly?* Grace was embarrassed how much she'd wanted and expected a long kiss goodnight.

In spite of the abrupt good-bye, the night had been magical. All night she was sure Matt was feeling the same way. Maybe thoughts of Faith came into his mind as he drove her home, maybe he was feeling sad that she *wasn't* Faith, that as much as he wanted to have a woman back in his life, he was realizing no one would be able to take her place.

Matt drove home elated. He thought the date couldn't have gone any better. He smiled remembering some of their conversation. His heart swelled remembering what it was like holding her close while they danced. It'd been difficult to restrain himself at the end of the night. He wanted to pull her into his arms and kiss her passionately, reluctant to let the night end at all.

But this relationship was too important to him—he wanted to do it right. He wanted to make sure Grace knew how precious she was to him, that it was more than just physical desire. He felt like a teenager, he couldn't wait to talk to her in the morning. *How early would be too early to call?*

The phone ringing woke Grace from a deep sleep. She didn't want to wake up, she was dreaming that she and Matt were married and that his warm body lay next to her's.

"Hello," Grace answered groggily.

"Tell me every detail!" Annie implored.

Grace described their perfect night. Not leaving out any details. Annie sighed appreciatively at the romanticism of the evening.

"Oh Annie! I think I'm really and truly in love for the first time. I've never felt anything close to this. But as much as I don't want it to be true, I don't think he'll ever get over Faith, or ever stop comparing me to her and I know I fall short in every way."

Grace went on to describe how abruptly the date had ended, she was sure it must have been thoughts of Faith that brought on the change.

"I don't think so, Grace. Maybe he thought it was the right way to act."

"Well, *I* wasn't about doing the right thing. I'm sure Faith was as pure as the driven snow . . . she probably didn't even allow him to kiss her on their first date."

"Try not to obsess about Faith, Grace. She's been gone for over three years, I bet he thinks of her a lot less than you think he does."

As soon as Grace put the phone back in its cradle, it rang again.

"Good morning! I'm not calling too early, am I?"

"Good morning to you, too." Grace laid her head back on the pillow, relishing the sound of Matt's voice, deepened from sleep.

"I didn't wake you, did I?"

"I'm awake, I just haven't gotten my lazy fanny out of bed yet."

Matt pictured her, her curls spread across her pillow, her body still warm from sleep. Oh, how he'd love to be waking up next to her.

"Feel like going out for brunch with me and Ella?

"I'd like nothing better."

25

It was crazy how fast everything changed after that one weekend. The dynamics were different. There was no way of going back to the way it was. They made plans every weekend, with and without Ella.

Matt never missed giving Grace a big hug and kiss before leaving for work each morning and greeted her and Ella with kisses and hugs when he came home at night. Grace ate with them most every night, often staying until after Ella went to bed when she and Matt would snuggle on the couch and watch their favorite shows.

It was like being married without the sexual intimacy. It was obvious Matt was determined not to let their physical desire for each other go any further than he thought proper.

~ ~

Halloween was upon them before they knew it. They laughed at Ella's excitement to dress up. Her favorite movie was "Sleeping Beauty," so of course that's who Ella wanted to be. She insisted on wearing her costume several days before Halloween, strutting around the house, insisting they call her "Sweeping Booty" and never failing to call Matt her "Pwince Chah-ming."

Fortunately, on Halloween night she quickly grew tired of going from house to house asking for treats. Matt had to carry her the last few blocks. She fell asleep in his arms and he put her to bed without removing her costume.

~ ~

Even all these months later, Matt still wore his wedding ring, he still put a firm line on how far they'd go in their physical relationship. Wasn't he experiencing the same frustrations Grace was?

She shared her concerns with Annie, "I know I should feel honored that he hasn't tried to push me into having sex with him. It's appalling to admit, but I'm afraid it wouldn't take much pushing. Isn't that awful? You'd think I'd know better. But, I've never, *ever* felt anything close to what I feel for him. I feel safe. I wonder if he draws the line out of a sense of loyalty to Faith. Her pictures are everywhere, there isn't a room in the house that doesn't have her gorgeous face looking out at us. There's an especially beautiful picture of her on his nightstand, her face is the first face he sees in the morning and the last face he sees before he goes to sleep. And of course, he still wears his wedding ring. I have this eerie sense I'm sharing him with her. He is undoubtedly physically attracted to me, and I know it takes supreme willpower on his part to stop things when he thinks we're going too far, but . . ."

"Why can't you just tell him how you feel? Tell him his wedding ring makes you feel like you're sharing him. Surely, after all the time you've spent together you can be honest with him?"

"You're right. He's taking me out tonight. I'll say something, get it out there."

~ ~

Matt took them to one of their favorite places. After they were seated, and ordered their food, he reached over and took hold of both Grace's hands. "I don't know what I'd do without you, Grace." He searched her eyes, "Would you mind if I prayed?"

"I would love for you to pray," she whispered.

Without letting go of her hands, Matt lowered his head and closed his eyes.

"Father God, I thank You for the gift of Grace. I thank you for the love we share for Ella. I thank You for this opportunity to be out alone together to enjoy our meal and each other. May you bless this food to our bodies and our bodies to Your service. Amen."

"Amen." Grace echoed. She deliberately didn't let go of his hands. She twisted his wedding ring, looking at it, willing herself to ask about it. "Why do you still wear it?"

He lifted his gaze from their enjoined fingers, looking genuinely perplexed. "I've never given it a thought. It's been on my finger since the day Faith put it there and I've never had a reason to take it off." *Until now.*

"Oh." It wasn't exactly what Grace wanted to hear. But she took comfort in the fact that he never gave it a thought, which meant it was unlikely he was *deliberately* not taking it off.

"Does it bother you?"

"A little. I feel a little bit like I'm sharing you, like I'm dating a married man."

"Well, you're wrong. You aren't dating a married man. I'm very much a single man and I am very . . ." He made sure Grace's eyes met his before he continued ". . . very much in love with *you*."

It was the first time he'd told her he loved her, and Grace felt suddenly self-conscious, she blushed and lowered her eyes to escape the intensity of his gaze. Her heart leapt inside of her, *He loves me! He loves me! He called me his gift!*

She knew he was waiting for her to say she loved him, too. And she *did* love him, but the words just wouldn't come out. When the silence got awkward he changed the subject, telling her something Ella had said that morning that made her laugh out loud.

When Matt walked her up to her house, she stopped before she unlocked the door. She turned to face him and buried her face into the base of his neck. With her lips pressed against his warm, scented skin she shyly whispered, "I love you too, Matt. I really, really love you."

Matt used two fingers to tilt her face up to his. He didn't say anything, his eyes took in all the details of her beautiful face before settling on her slightly parted lips. With one hand on the small of her back and his other hand cupping the back of her head, he pulled her close against him and kissed her deeply. He stopped long enough to take her keys from her and unlocked the door—pushing it open and closing it before pulling her once again into a passionate embrace.

Their bodies strained together, trying to be as close as possible. They were both breathing heavily. He trailed small kisses along her neck before settling his mouth back on hers. Her knees felt weak, and he swept his arm under her legs and carried her as easily as if she were Ella. He sat on the couch, holding her on his lap, never taking his lips off of hers. He slipped off one of her shoes and caressed her ankle, slowly ran his hand to up over her calf, past her knee—she gasped at the pleasure his warm hand against her skin gave her. She slid her hand between the buttons of his shirt, feeling his heart thudding beneath the warm skin of his chest. He groaned and reached for the zipper on her dress, unzipping it in one fluid motion. He slid it off one silky shoulder, pressed his lips against the hollow of her collarbone, trailing kisses down to the lacy edge of her bra. She tugged his shirt loose from his pants and Matt suddenly stopped, took both her hands in his. "We need to stop," he said raggedly. He lifted her gently off of him, settling her on the couch before standing up. With his back to her, he tucked his shirt back into his pants and raked his hands through his hair.

Grace self consciously pulled the sleeve of her dress back onto her shoulder. "Okay," Grace whispered." *But it's not okay, I* ***didn't*** *want it to stop. I* ***wouldn't*** *have stopped you.*

Matt inhaled deeply before finally turning back around to face her. "I'm sorry, Grace. I promise I won't let it go that far again. You mean too much to me, I want your first time to be everything it . . ." His voice trailed off.

Grace's heart sunk. *He thinks I'm a virgin! How will he feel when I tell him I'm not?* Grace had pushed all the unpleasant memories of her past into the deep recesses or her mind, but now they came rushing back—the debilitating guilt and self-incrimination threatened to cut off her very breath. She couldn't escape from her past after all. She couldn't let Matt believe she was something she wasn't. He deserved better. She had to tell him. Not tonight, with their heightened passions, but soon.

He pulled her up into his arms, deftly zipped her dress back up. He held her face in his hands, "I love you, Grace. You have no idea how much I love you. I want to do things right, I want God's blessing on our relationship."

Before Grace could respond, he kissed her softly and walked out the door.

As soon as the door closed, the tears began to fall. Grace had messed up too much to get God's blessing on their relationship. Hadn't she always known that? She was sullied. Because she hadn't remained pure like Faith or Annie she was going to lose the best thing that ever happened to her.

She knew for the first time what a real broken heart felt like. The pain she'd felt when Chad betrayed her was nothing compared to the pain she felt now. She didn't think she'd ever get to sleep with the weight of sadness pressing so heavily on her chest. The sun was coming up before she finally slipped into a fitful sleep.

She woke up with the same sick feeling.

She called Matt and told him she didn't feel like going to church with them.

He called after church to see if she felt like getting something to eat.

"No. I better pass. I'm still not feeling myself. I'm sure I just need rest. I'm going to try to sleep, so it's probably better if you don't stop by or call me. I'll see you in the morning."

She could hear the disappointment in Matt's voice, but she couldn't bear the thought of facing him today.

26

She dreaded having to tell him the things she'd done and who she'd been. He'd be appalled at the ease with which she'd allowed a relationship to evolve into sexual intimacy. She shuddered to think how awful it would be to be married to Chad. God had saved her from a shallow, selfish man. If only she could have trusted there was someone like Matt out there, maybe she could have waited.

Monday morning came, and Matt opened the door to greet her before she even had a chance to knock. "How's my sweet Grace feeling this morning?" He held her at arms length, "She's looking as beautiful as ever." He pulled her to him and kissed the top of her head.

Grace smiled weakly and said she was feeling a tad better. Matt poured her a cup of coffee and handed it to her with his left hand, holding the cup out of her grasp long enough for her to see he wasn't wearing his wedding ring.

How happy it would have made her if the deep shame and feelings of inadequacy hadn't resurfaced and convinced her she wasn't worthy of Matt's love.

She forced herself to smile, but couldn't think of anything to say. He gave her his broad grin, "Just wanted you to know I am a single man, very much in love with a very special girl."

He pulled her to him, gave her a longer kiss goodbye than normal. "I'll call you later, have a good day."

"You, too."

Grace sat numbly down on the chair, her head in her hands. Oh, how she dreaded telling Matt about her past. But she wouldn't keep it from him.

She called Kate and asked her if she'd babysit so she and Matt could be alone tonight. She would insist they go to a restaurant they'd never been to before. She didn't want to taint the sweet memories of any of their favorites.

She crept into Ella's room. Staring down at her sweet face. What if Matt was so hurt and disillusioned by what she'd done that he no longer wanted her to watch Ella? How could she stand not being a part of this precious baby's life?

It'd been little more than a year, yet Grace couldn't imagine loving her own child more than she loved Ella. If Matt did want her to stay on, would the pain of seeing him every day, loving him like she did, yet knowing they didn't have a future together, ever go away?

She sat down in the rocker, slowly rocking, lost in thought. How many times had she rocked Ella in this chair, read her books and cuddled with her before her naps? Kissed her sweet cheeks and took in the sweet smell of her?

She turned to look at the now familiar picture of Faith holding Ella. She stopped rocking. The picture was gone. She got up and walked into the bedroom, the picture of Faith that had sat on his nightstand had been replaced with a snapshot of the three of *them*.

She picked it up and studied it. It was taken at the pool. Their cheeks were pink from the sun, the breeze had blown one of Grace's curls against her face. She remembered it being taken but hadn't known Matt had gotten the roll of film developed. Matt held Ella in one arm, his other arm around Grace, his hand gently clasping her bare waist.

Tears came unbidden to her eyes. She couldn't fathom her life without them. This past year had been the happiest time of her life.

She walked into the front hall; their wedding picture had been taken down as well. He'd taken down *every* photo of Faith. He'd made an obvious effort to show Grace he was serious about her taking Faith's place in his life. The sweet gesture made Grace dread telling Matt about her past all the more.

When he called later in the afternoon to check on her, she was unnaturally quiet, reticent about talking about their plans for the evening.

"Is something bothering you, Grace?"

"Actually, there is."

Matt felt a twinge of anxiety. *Had she decided it was too soon to declare their love for each other?* He waited for her to continue.

She closed her eyes and sighed. "I need to tell you something. Something that will probably change the way you feel about me. I want to tell you tonight. It's not fair to keep it from you any longer. I already called Kate, and she agreed to come over to watch Ella."

Matt thought she sounded close to tears, but he sensed she wanted to talk to him face to face so he didn't keep her on the phone.

He couldn't concentrate on his work—he couldn't get their short conversation off his mind.

How could she possibly think she could tell him something about herself that would change his feelings for her? He was in too deep. He couldn't envision his life without her in it.

The minutes felt like hours, he was still feeling uneasy when he pulled into the driveway.

Ella ran to greet him with her usual enthusiasm, but Grace held back awkwardly, not even making eye contact. Her odd behavior made him more apprehensive than ever to hear what she had to tell him.

She hugged and kissed Ella good-bye.

"It won't take me long to get ready. Kate should be here any minute."

"I'll be at your house in less than half an hour."

Before Grace could slip away he pulled her into a tight hug and whispered into her ear, "Whatever it is that is bothering you, I know I can make it better."

His words brought tears to her eyes. "I don't think you can," she whispered into his neck before slipping out of his arms and out the door, she didn't want him to see her tears.

27

Grace suggested a restaurant that had private booths where it was unlikely they'd be overheard. Her voice was disconsolately resigned.

"My goodness, Grace! Your melancholy is rubbing off on me. Where did it come from? I drove home feeling elated Saturday night, sure our relationship had hit an important milestone. We said we loved each other. I thought it meant something. I can't imagine what could've made things change so drastically from Saturday until today."

Grace looked straight ahead, saying softly, "You'll understand when I tell you."

The rest of the ride to the restaurant was quiet. Neither of them said a word.

As soon as they were seated, Matt reached for Grace's hands. She didn't entwine her fingers with his, they remained motionless in his. He grasped them more tightly, implored her to look at him. When she raised her head there were tears in her eyes.

"I can't tell you what I need to tell you holding hands with you."

Matt reluctantly released her hands. She put them under the table and nervously started tearing her paper napkin into tiny pieces.

He released a sigh, "Okay. Talk."

Grace took a deep breath, willing herself to keep her composure and tell him every detail.

"Please don't say anything until I've told you everything, okay?"

Matt nodded in assent.

She started with the college party. She ended with the betrayal of her friend and boyfriend. She didn't leave anything out. She didn't defend her behavior, only expressed her shame and remorse.

The whole time she talked Matt didn't take his eyes off of hers. He had a slight frown, but his eyes were inscrutable. She had no idea what he was thinking.

When she finally finished, she let the tears flow. "So you see," she sniffled, "I'm not the girl you think I am. I'm nothing like your perfect Faith."

Matt slipped out of the booth and squeezed in next to her. When she didn't look at him, he gently turned her face towards his, kissed her tears, pressed soft kisses all over her face, before finally settling his lips over hers.

When he lifted his head, her eyes remained downcast.

"Look at me, Grace."

She slowly lifted her eyes to meet his.

"I'm sorry you had to experience all that crap. I wish I could meet those jerks, I'd like to punch their lights out for treating you the way they did. That first joker should be rotting in a jail cell somewhere."

Grace allowed a slight smile to break through her tears at his protective bravado. A weight lifted from her chest but she needed him to understand she wasn't innocent.

"I made those choices. I knew better. I ignored the still, small voice of His Spirit and now I am being punished."

"Didn't your church teach the parts of the Bible that talk about forgiveness? About grace?"

"They did, but they also taught about consequences. Chastening. Reaping what you sow and all that. And . . . goads."

"Goads?"

"Yeah, you know, the rods the shepherds used to whack their sheep back onto the right path."

"Is that how you picture our Good Shepherd, who knows us each by name? *Whacking* us onto to the right path? Goodness, Grace. That's a twisted view of a loving Shepherd."

"All I know is I've always believed the 'whacking' will never end. I've never *felt* forgiven. Never felt I deserved it."

"No one 'deserves' it. What about His promise to remove our sin as far as the east is from the west? What about the part that promises if we confess our sins He is faithful and just to forgive us our sins? Are those just empty words to you? Believe me, they aren't empty words to me. I've done things that have required plenty of forgiveness. One of the greatest things that separates Christianity from all other religions is grace and forgiveness."

Grace's heart leapt with renewed hope. *He isn't judging me! He isn't disgusted with me! He believes I've been cleansed from all unrighteousness because of Christ's righteousness. If only I can believe those words and* ***feel*** *cleansed.*

Grace dropped her gaze back to the table. "Deep down I always believed I couldn't escape my consequences. It was willful sin. I can't help but compare myself to Faith. She sounds so perfect. And then Saturday night, when you inferred it would be my first time, my heart sunk. I figured when you found out it *wasn't* going to be my first time it would shatter your good girl image of me and you wouldn't want to . . ."

Matt interrupted her, "First of all, Faith was *not* perfect, nobody is. If you *were* perfect, you wouldn't be normal and you'd bore me senseless."

Grace couldn't help but laugh.

"Secondly, guess what? It's not gonna be *my* first time either."

"Well, *duh*."

"No, I mean it wasn't even my first time with Faith. She never knew that, and I regretted never telling her. Like you, I was afraid if she knew, it might diminish the man she thought I was. She made such a big deal out of it. Having that secret meant missing college reunions, dropping college friendships because I was paranoid the truth might come out. It meant I deflected all her questions about my college years, even though there were a lot of funny stories I knew she could appreciate. She often mentioned how much it meant to her that we were each other's first and I was too much of a coward to correct her. I hated having that secret. So I can understand you not wanting to keep your past from me. It isn't healthy to keep secrets from each other."

Grace didn't say anything, just nodded, hoping he would feel free to share *his* story.

He took a deep breath before continuing, "I was a freshman, kind of cocky, a little taken aback by all the female attention I was getting. At my first party, a beautiful girl didn't leave my side. She laughed at everything I said. She deliberately rubbed herself against me. I'd never felt more physically attracted to anyone in my life. She asked me back to her room and I foolishly agreed, knowing I'd drank too much and my hormones were raging. She pulled me into her room and we collapsed on the bed, she didn't waste anytime getting her clothes off and I had hard time not gawking. It was the first time I'd ever seen a girl completely naked. When she started unbuckling my belt, sanity hit me and I tried to slow it down. She took a condom out of her nightstand and handed it to me. I asked myself, *is it really such a big deal?* This obviously wasn't *her* first Rodeo, and I didn't have to worry about getting her pregnant. And, the weird part was, *now* I was afraid it would hurt her feelings if I refused."

Matt briefly closed his eyes, breathed out a disappointed sigh. "When it was done, I wanted out of there. I was self-conscious about being naked in front of her. I gathered my clothes and forced myself to walk to the bathroom with a slow strut, when what I wanted to do was cover myself up and run."

Grace bit back a smile, Matt had such an easy confidence, it was difficult to imagine him ever feeling self-conscious.

Matt continued his story, "When I came out of the bathroom with my clothes on, she was still naked on the bed, splayed out, not remotely self-conscious. She knew she had a spectacular body and didn't want me to forget it. I thought the image of her naked body on that bed would be imprinted on my mind for the rest of my life. I just met the girl! How could I have shared something so intimate with her?"

Grace nodded in understanding, willing him to continue.

"I felt sick to my stomach. I didn't know anything about her. I could barely remember her name. I found myself looking at anything *but* her. I wandered around her room looking at her pictures and books, hoping she'd put her clothes on while I wasn't looking. She didn't. I finally made up some excuse to get out of there and left without a backward glance. I worried she'd think what we did made us a couple, and she did. She waited for me after my classes, made sure we were at the cafeteria at the same time, wanted to meet at the library to study together. The more time I spent with her the more I realized how shallow she was, we'd never be a match. I tried avoiding her, but she had my schedule memorized. Finally, I had to tell her, as gently as I could, that I needed some space. She cried and claimed I'd used her. I got through college without getting close to any other girls. I hardly went on any dates."

He took her hands in his and squeezed them, "See Grace? I messed up, too. The difference is I *feel* forgiven and I finally forgave myself."

A smile played at the corner of her lips and the tension left her shoulders. Joy bubbled up in her chest. The anxiety of the last few days had been for naught. Because of God's abounding love and mercy, she wasn't sullied in Matt's eyes. He could love her in spite of her past. *And* he shared things with her he'd never even shared with Faith. Could she dare hope they could make it work? That they could love each other forever?

Matt exhaled deeply, "So . . .any thoughts? I know that was a lot to lay on you."

Ridiculously, Grace wanted to ask him if he still had the image of the beautiful naked body in his mind. *What was wrong with her?* Not only could she torment herself with comparisons to Faith, now she wondered how often this beautiful girl from years ago popped into his head.

She pushed her stupid thoughts aside and forced herself to smile. "Thank you for sharing all that with me. It *is* freeing not having secrets."

She looked down at their enjoined hands. Not for the first time she thought what beautiful hands he had. She thought about how the touch of those hands made her feel. She looked at the faint line of white where his wedding ring had been.

"How did you meet Faith?"

"Not long after I graduated, I met Faith in a restaurant and knew I wanted to marry her. On one of our first dates she asked me if I'd ever had a girlfriend. The honest answer? 'No, but . . .'

She didn't let me continue, clapped her hands in delight. I was her first boyfriend too! 'Wasn't it amazing? God 'saved' us for each other.' I couldn't disappoint her, Grace. Everything about her delighted me, I didn't want to lose her and reasoned since it was just the *one* time, it didn't really count. But it *always* bothered me. I hated keeping that secret. Every time she'd tell the story about us being each other's 'firsts,' my stomach knotted up, I pled with God to never let her find out she *wasn't* my first."

Matt's voice became thick with emotion, "Turns out, God answered that prayer . . . she never did find out."

Grace's heart hurt for him, and she squeezed his hands in sympathy.

"I'm sorry you lost the love of your life. I worry I'll never be able to take her place."

"Please don't say that Grace. I did love her more than life. After she died, I didn't want to live. I didn't know how to care for my own child. I thought of poor Ella as more of a burden than a gift. How could a father feel that way? I worried something was wrong with me. I was convinced I'd never find another woman to take her place. I was sure I was going to be a single dad the rest of my life, but maybe I could make Ella my life, maybe I could make up for all those months I hardly held her or tried to bond with her. I swear to you, the first time I felt the slightest attraction for another woman was the morning you showed up to watch Ella. As the weeks went by and my attraction to you grew, I tried telling myself it was only because it'd been so long since I'd even *looked* at a pretty woman. But we became friends, and I started caring about you. I wanted to know everything about you, spend every minute I could with you. I couldn't believe how jealous I was when that guy asked you out. I thought maybe I'd blown my chance with you."

Grace smiled, "And *you* cannot imagine how devastated *I* was that I already had a date."

"And then the weirdest thing started happening. *You* became the woman in my dreams. All these years I treasured the nights when Faith appeared in my dreams. She was so real in them, I'd wake up with tears in my eyes."

Grace's eyes dropped back to the table.

"Doesn't that mean something to you, Grace? *You* took her place in my dreams."

Something else occurred to him, another first. "And you know what else? Faith's birthday is coming up. Every year I've dreaded that day. She always loved her birthday, loved making a big deal made out of it. The sadness of not being able to spoil her on that day overwhelmed me every year. But guess what? I'm not dreading it this year. I'm not dreading it because I have so much to be thankful for, I have you and Ella and every day I look forward to coming home to you both."

Grace's heart began to race. ***My** birthday is coming up. Please, please don't let me have to share a birthday with her too. Not her husband **and** her birthday.* "When's her birthday?" Grace asked.

"December 15th."

"No way." Grace didn't smile. A knot formed in her stomach. "That's my birthday, too."

Shucks, Matt thought. He wanted Grace to have her own day, she deserved her own day. He hated that she was always comparing herself to Faith. He didn't know how to convince her it never occurred to him to compare them. They were so completely different.

Matt sighed deeply and stood up, took her hands and pulled her up and into his arms. He held her tightly against him, spoke softly into her hair, "Please Grace, I want you to stop comparing yourself to Faith." He lifted her head so he could look in her eyes. "I've tried every way I know to make you understand how uniquely special you are to me."

"I know you have, it's just . . ."

"Picture my brain as a closet. There are lots of boxes in the closet. Faith is in a very special box, but it's in the back of the closet. Sometimes it's even hard to remember all that's in that box. Recently a new box was added. It's not in the back of the closet, it's in the front. It's a wondrous big box, it almost takes up the *entire* closet. *You're* that box and it's filled with all the things I love about you. Does that make any sense? Does that help?"

Her green eyes glittered with tears, "Thank you. It does help."

He gently kissed her, "Good, because I don't want you wasting any more time obsessing about Faith and feeling like you can't ever measure up." He smiled, "Do we have a deal?"

Grace couldn't help but return his smile. "Deal." And at that moment she really did believe she was going to keep up her end of the bargain.

"Great, now let's get outta here."

He pulled her close to his side as they walked out, protecting her from the blustery, cold wind. Winter would be here before they knew it. He started the car to let it warm up and then turned and pulled her into a close embrace.

"Oh, Grace," he whispered huskily. "I will never stop thanking God for bringing you into our lives. I love you."

"And I love you," she whispered back.

Matt was quiet on the drive home, marveling at God's goodness. God hadn't intended for him to spend the rest of his life alone, after all. Grace was perfect for him in every way. Not to mention a perfect mother for Ella. It was hard to fathom it had been just a little over a year since she'd shown up at his doorstep.

28

Thanksgiving was right around the corner. Matt was eager to meet Grace's parents and suggested they come out and spend a few days with them. He offered to buy them airline tickets and much to Grace's surprise, they accepted his offer.

Grace was a little nervous about the meeting. Her parents lived such a quiet, secluded life that she thought the boisterousness of Matt's family might intimidate them. She needn't have worried. Her parents were enchanted with Ella, connected immediately with Matt's parents and laughed heartily at the competitive ribbing that went on between Matt and his brothers.

Matt's family lived several hours away, so he didn't see them as much as he'd like. But they made up for it on holidays.

They treated Grace just like family the first time they met her. She loved listening to their stories. It made her wish all the more she'd grown up with brothers and sisters of her own.

Matt had an ulterior motive for wanting Grace's parents to join them on Thanksgiving. He wanted to ask Grace's father for permission to marry his daughter. He managed to get him alone the first night they were there and her poor father had gotten all choked up. He told Matt they thought he was perfect for their Grace and that they'd been praying it would happen.

Grace knew her parents were exhausted after Thanksgiving dinner and insisted they needn't help clean up. She asked them to drive her car back to her house and let Matt bring her home later.

When the last dish was washed and everything put back in its place, Matt and Grace fell onto the sofa. Grace sat on one end and Matt pulled her feet onto his lap, insisting on giving her a foot rub.

"You poor thing, you were on your feet way too much today. But, hey, we pulled it off, didn't we?"

"We sure did," Grace sighed. The day couldn't have been more perfect.

"Your parents are wonderful, Grace. You haven't talked much about them and I wondered if it might be because they were a bit odd or something. But they are genuine, loving people. Obviously crazy about you and obviously still in love with each other."

"They used to kind of embarrass me, to tell you the truth. It always made me feel good to see how much they loved each other and I never doubted they loved me with everything they had, but sometimes I thought they were too narrow-minded and old fashioned. I saw them in a different light after I came home from New York. For the first time I appreciated their steadfast love and great faith."

"Well they sure did raise a wonderful daughter. I loved hearing all the stories about you as a little girl."

"I was an introverted little nerd, that's for sure. Unlike *you.* From everything I heard, there wasn't *anything* that could bring you down. I loved the story of you coming home from first grade being so proud of yourself for being 'the best reader in the worst group.' I can just see it." Grace laughed remembering it.

"You were never a little 'nerd.' Just a funny, shy, beautiful little girl."

"Hmmm. I don't know. My mom said from babyhood on, I took in every detail of everyone I met. She was forever telling me how rude it was to stare at people."

"Sort of how I couldn't stop staring at you at the coffee shop that first day?"

"No, nothing like that. Besides, you were only staring at my eyes because they're so much like Ella's. No, I definitely had a serious staring problem. My junior high school years were the worst. I remember waiting to get picked up from school one day and watching a couple of kids making out in the corner. By the way I stood there taking in every detail of all the kissing and groping, you would have thought they were out there performing just for me. In the midst of my enthrallment, the 'performance' came to an abrupt halt and the 'starlet' walked menacingly over to me. She got about two inches from my face and told me I should 'take a picture, it will last longer.' I was mortified."

Matt laughed, sliding her feet off his lap and pulling her close. Still smiling, he looked down at her, "You *are* a funny one, Grace Ryan. Just one of the many reasons I'm so crazy about you."

"Anyway, once I became friends with Annie in high school she had more than enough personalty for both of us. I started to come out of my shell a little bit."

"Well, I love you just the way you are...quirks and all. I remember the day I told my mom I thought I might be falling for Ella's nanny. I think she worried I'd never get married again, and she couldn't wait to meet you. They think you're perfect for me and Ella. A beautiful answer to their prayers."

"When I went home last Christmas, my parents could sense you were becoming more than just a friend to me, but the sweet things kept themselves from prying too much. You'd never made me feel like I was anything more than Ella's nanny, so I wasn't about to admit that I thought I might be falling for you." Grace almost added that she'd also told them no one would ever be able to replace Faith, but she remembered her promise to him, and bit back the words. "Today, I could see how happy they were for me. Oh, and did they ever get a kick out of Ella! She already has them wrapped around her little finger."

They cuddled and kissed until it was time to drive Grace home. Matt prayed he wouldn't have to endure many more nights without her in his bed. How long could it take to plan a wedding, anyway?

29

Matt wanted December 15th to be a doubly important day for Grace, her birthday *and* the day he asked her to marry him. He hoped this would help her forget the fact that she shared a birthday with Faith.

Grace could tell Matt was trying hard to make her birthday extra special. She knew it was a tough decision not to acknowledge it was Faith's birthday, too. But bless his heart, he decided to make the day all about Grace.

He was taking her to an especially nice place for dinner. It was one of the few places they'd never been. He encouraged her to go out and shop for a special dress. Annie went with her, determined to help her find the perfect dress. They found a navy halter cut dress that showed off Grace's shoulders. It fit her like a glove, nipping in at her small waist and falling just a few inches below the knee. A silver rhinestone button enclosed the neck. They found beautiful, shimmering rhinestone earrings and a matching bracelet to wear with it.

Grace took her time getting ready that night and when she looked at her reflection in the mirror she couldn't help but smile. She knew Matt would be impressed.

When Matt knocked at the door, Grace was ready for him. She opened the door and they stood and gawked at each other for a minute. Grace had never seen Matt look more handsome. His dark chocolate brown eyes shone with appreciation. His black suit hugged his shoulders. His hair was still slightly damp from his shower, a lock of it stubbornly falling across his forehead.

Grace had pulled her curls into a loose side ponytail, because she wanted to show off the rhinestone button and her sparkly earrings.

"Wow! You look spectacular, Grace." He held her hand up and she did a perfect pirouette to show off every angle.

"You look pretty spectacular yourself," Grace said softly.

As they drove to the restaurant, Matt couldn't stop himself from stealing glances at her. She really was gorgeous.

He couldn't wait to put that engagement ring on her finger. It was a one and a half karat, square cut diamond set in white gold. It would perfectly set off her silver jewelry and rhinestone clasp.

Since he'd wanted to surprise her, he'd picked out the ring without any input from her. He figured she could get something different if she didn't like it, but something told him she'd think it was perfect.

When they walked into the restaurant, a small band was just setting up.

"Oh, good!" Grace exclaimed excitedly. "It'll be fun to dance. It'll remind me of our first date, dancing out on the patio."

Matt hoped she'd remember the first song they'd danced to that night, he'd checked ahead of time to see if it was in the band's repertoire. He planned on it being the first song they'd dance to tonight, too.

Except this time, when the song ended he would be dropping to one knee and asking for her hand in marriage. He didn't want to wait until the end of the night to ask her. He wanted to celebrate as early as he could and into the wee hours of the morning.

Matt ordered a nice bottle of wine. They talked and laughed while the band played.

When the band struck the first chords of the song they'd danced to all those months ago, Matt could tell by the smile on Grace's face that she remembered.

"Shall we dance?" Matt offered his hand.

"Most certainly. How perfect is this? They're playing the very first song we danced to!"

Matt couldn't stop grinning as he led her out to the floor.

He held her close as they swayed to the music, silently thanking God for bringing her into his life, in His perfect timing.

Grace placed her hand on Matt's chest. Unlike their first date, they kept their eyes locked on each other as they slowly swayed to the music. She'd never felt such deep contentment. It felt so good to be held in his arms, remembering their first date, marveling at how far God had brought them. She didn't want the song to end. But it did, and as they pulled apart, Matt dropped down onto one knee.

Grace's heart skipped a beat, her face became hot. *Was he really going to ask her to marry him? Here? On the dance floor?*

He produced the ring, "Will you marry me, Grace?"

Her throat was too constricted to talk, tears filled her eyes as she nodded an emphatic "yes."

He slipped the ring on her finger and then stood up, locked his gaze on hers. "I love you with every fiber of my being, Grace. I want to spend the rest of my life proving to you how much I love you."

They embraced and the whole restaurant clapped in appreciation.

Matt whispered suggestively into her ear, "And I can't wait to start making Ella some brothers and sisters."

30

Annie was predictably over the moon with the news and eager to help plan every detail of the wedding.

They poured over bride's magazines and shopped for dresses. Grace tried on dozens, determined to find the perfect one. But before she made the final decision, Grace wanted to make sure her dress wouldn't look anything like Faith's. She couldn't remember exactly what Faith's looked like, but she knew she could find their wedding album down in the basement in Faith's memory box.

While Ella took her nap she headed down to look through the pictures. Evidently Faith had not been a very organized person; photos, letters and albums were stuffed in any old way.

She couldn't keep herself from looking at some of the cards and letters from Matt that Faith had saved and couldn't help but feel pangs of jealousy; they really had had something special. She could only hope and pray theirs would be just as special.

She didn't want to ask Matt about Faith's dress. He still got prickly when she asked questions about her. He told her whether she was aware of it or not, her whole demeanor changed when they discussed her.

Grace got so engrossed in the photos, she forgot all about Ella sleeping upstairs, which was not a good thing, because it didn't take long for Ella to get into some serious mischief.

She looked carefully at each picture in the wedding album. Fortunately, Faith wore a dress that would never appeal to Grace. There wasn't a chance she'd pick one remotely like it.

Their wedding had been less than seven years ago, yet Matt had aged. He had a few gray hairs now, and the grooves in his cheeks were deeper. The loss of Faith had aged him, but in Grace's eyes, he'd only gotten better looking.

Grace glanced at her watch, startled by how long she'd been down there. Ella was probably awake by now. She hurriedly started stuffing everything back in the box. Just as she was getting the last of it in, she noticed a frayed piece of notebook paper stuck against the side. She pulled it out, and her first thought was, *how in the world did my birth mother's prayer get into Faith's memory box?*

But of course, she knew better, she knew exactly where her copy of the prayer was. It was carefully folded in her wallet. How could this be? Why would Faith have it, too? How did she get it? She remembered the eerie similarities between the two of them, they had the same birthday, they were both adopted—her heart froze at the realization.

They were twins, separated at birth. She couldn't marry Matt. It would be, well . . . incestuous. She kept reading and re-reading the prayer. She put her head in her hands and cried. It had been cruel to separate twin sisters.

Who would do such a thing? After meeting Janet, she was *sure* she wasn't in on it. Plus, the prayer only referenced *one* baby.

Did her parents know? Were the Davidsons in on it? One thing she knew for certain was that Janet's husband knew. She'd told Grace he was the one that delivered her. That's how they'd met. Why did he let Janet believe she'd only had one baby? Why did he keep that secret from her all these years? What would have happened if Faith and Grace had both decided to reach out to Janet?

Still gripping the paper in her hand, Grace sat and wept.

31

Matt came home, calling out for his "girls." When no one answered, he became alarmed. He heard Ella in her room, and when she saw him, she ran to him with her usual welcoming enthusiasm. She was covered with baby powder; every thing in the room was covered with baby powder. It was a mess. Where was Grace? He felt the same heart-stopping fear he'd felt when he couldn't find Faith.

"Where's Momma Grace?" he asked Ella urgently.

Ella clearly didn't know or care. She wanted to show him how she'd changed Baby's diaper.

Matt became even more alarmed, knowing Grace would never leave Ella unattended for the amount of time it must have taken for her to wreak this much destruction.

"Grace!" Matt called out louder. As he walked from room to room, he thought he heard something down in the basement and rushed down there.

He found her sitting beside Faith's memory box, with a note in her hand. It ticked him off. She'd needlessly scared him. And what was she doing looking through Faith's memory box?

He'd had it with her obsession with Faith. She'd *promised* him she wouldn't go there anymore, and now here she was, digging through

Faith's personal stuff, undoubtedly finding more ways she didn't measure up.

"What are you doing?" he began angrily. "Do you have *any* idea what Ella's been up to?"

He noticed she was crying, tears running down her face, her make-up smeared.

"I can't marry you after all," Grace said softly, between sniffles.

"What *now*?" he asked harshly. He was done with coaxing and wheedling her into believing God brought them together for a reason. He wasn't doing it anymore.

When she didn't immediately answer, he said, "Fine. I've had it, Grace. I've had it with all the questions and comparisons. I've had it trying to convince you that I think you're perfect for me."

Grace was so stunned by his angry tone she stopped crying, getting a little miffed herself. "Don't you even care what I found? The *reason* I can't marry you?"

Grace hadn't expected this, she'd expected him to console her, to try and convince her she was wrong—she didn't recognize this angry, impatient Matt.

"No, I don't. I don't give a damn what you found. You're forever going to dig and compare. There will never be an end to it. I'm done." He turned on his heel, and started walking away.

"Matt, wait!"

Matt stopped and turned around. Grace had her arm stretched out holding a piece of paper. Her hand was shaking. "Please. Just read it."

He took it from her, glanced at it, he didn't need to read it. He knew what it was.

"So, what? It's a sweet memento Faith kept since she was a little girl. It was from her birth mother, whom, as you know, she never even met."

"Don't you remember me telling you how I found that note from my birth mother? Don't you remember me telling you it's how I found out I was adopted? This is the *exact* prayer I found! Faith and I have the same birthday! We were both adopted. Don't you get it?"

She started sniffling again, "Faith and I are sisters!"

Matt got goosebumps. He went over and squatted down beside her, gently wiped a tear from her cheek. "Oh, honey," he said softly. "This is incredible. A true miracle. Amazing! Only an all powerful God could have arranged to bring you . . ."

"Well, it doesn't amaze me!" she rudely interrupted. "It makes me sick. It's creepy to think about marrying my *sister's* husband. I won't do it."

Her sharp tone and stony refusal to see any good, caused the tenderness he'd just felt turn back into frustrated anger. He stood back up. "If that's really how you really feel, then go ahead and leave. And once you go out that door, don't even think about coming back. I won't let you play with Ella's heart the way you've been playing with mine."

Grace was so shocked and hurt by his quick capitulation, she retaliated with matching anger, "You can't keep Ella from me. I'm her . . . her *aunt!*"

"Oh, really? I think any court in the land would think a father has a *little* more say-so than an aunt, and if I say I don't want you coming back, then you *won't* be coming back."

"How could you even *think* about doing that to Ella? I'm as a much of a parent to her as you are!"

"She needs someone who won't walk out of our life over a stupid piece of paper. It's not what I want, and Ella deserves better."

"A stupid piece of paper? I can't believe you're being this insensitive!" she said hotly. "You're asking me to *leave*? Right after I make this shocking, devastating discovery? Learning I have a sister I never knew about and that she was married to ***you***?"

"What do you expect from me? You say you won't marry me. Why would I want you hanging around?"

"Fine!" Grace stood up, violently pushed him out of her way. "You don't have to ask *me* twice. And here . . . I guess I won't be needing this!" She twisted her ring off and threw it at him.

She got to the top of stairs just as Ella rounded the corner, covered in powder from head to toe. She could hear Matt down in the basement kicking stuff around.

Grace's heart caught in her chest. How would she be able to bear not being a part of Ella's life? She would *find* a way to be in it, regardless of how Matt felt about her.

Grace could barely talk without crying, she bent down to Ella's level. "I have to go now, sweetheart. Can you come give me a hug?"

Ella ran to her, clinging to her longer than usual. Grace wondered if Ella sensed her tension, her crushing sadness.

When Grace finally stood up, she was covered with powder, too. She would forever associate the smell of baby powder with leaving this precious little girl and the man she'd grown to love with all her being.

Grace walked slowly out to her car, half expecting Matt to run after her, begging her to see reason. But he didn't. She sat in her car a few minutes before starting the engine and heading home.

She let herself into her house with a heavy heart.

She stared at the phone, willing it to ring. Matt calling to apologize. But it didn't ring. She sat there for hours. Was he really willing to let her go without a fight?

Maybe if she left town for a while he'd see he couldn't live without her, beg her to come back.

She called the airline and booked a flight for the following morning.

She half-heartedly grabbed a few articles of clothing and put them in an overnight bag. She kept expecting the phone to ring and hear Matt's beloved deep voice asking her to forgive him for being so impatient with her.

She couldn't sleep. She kept reliving their argument. Matt had been so angry, and his anger had cut her to the quick. Was it the hurt that made her lash out like she did? What must he think of her *throwing* her engagement ring at him?

It was almost time to leave for the airport. She couldn't leave without hearing his voice. She swallowed her pride and dialed his number.

He answered impatiently, and when he heard her voice, he was silent, waiting for her to continue.

"I, um, just wanted to tell you . . . I booked a flight to go see my parents. I actually have to leave in just a few minutes . . . I thought maybe . . ."

"That sounds like a good idea, Grace. I hope you have a good trip." He hung up on her without saying another word.

He hung up on her! Grace was shocked. She'd never known him to be rude. She didn't think he was capable of treating her that coldly. Fear clutched her heart, was this really going to be the end? Could their first real argument destroy a love she'd begun to believe was rock solid?

32

After she collected her boarding pass and headed to her gate, she tried convincing herself Matt was on his way to the airport. He would run down the concourse, stop her from getting on the plane minutes before they closed the door, just like in the movies.

She sat in the boarding area, waiting until the last minute to board. They gave the final boarding call. She sat through it, stayed in her seat and watched the airplane back away from the gate.

As she sat there, feeling dejected and alone, she remembered the last time she'd felt this desolate. After being betrayed and leaving a job she loved, she'd begged God to show Himself to her. She wanted Him to be as real to her as He was to Annie. She remembered how she'd thought He'd answered her when she found the prayer from her birth mother.

It suddenly dawned on her how mightily He'd answered *all* her prayers. Abundantly, exceedingly more than she could have hoped for or imagined. Only an all knowing, loving God could have arranged all the pieces to fall together to lead her to a sister she'd never known about and a niece who needed a loving mother. She felt tremors at the realization of the magnitude of the miracle The Prayer had wrought.

The insecurities she'd felt about Faith were replaced with feelings of genuine love. Now she mourned the fact she'd never known her. Now she wanted to know everything about her. She wanted to know the things that made Matt love her so. She wanted Ella to know all about her, too. She didn't want Ella to ever forget how much Faith had longed for her and loved her.

And Matt.

Unlike her, he'd immediately recognized the miracle. *What had he said? He called it a "true miracle."*

Had she really blown it? Was Matt really done with her, as he'd claimed? She couldn't lose him. She would crawl back to him, beg for his forgiveness. *Please Lord, forgive me for not recognizing Your hand in this. Please let Matt forgive me.*

She sighed and grabbed her suitcase, walking slowly back through the terminal. As she approached the exit, she spotted Matt, leaning casually against the wall, one heel pressed to the wall, arms crossed, a big grin on his face.

Joy surged through her at the sight of him, but she forced herself not to smile.

She wanted to run into his arms. But her stubborn pride wouldn't let her. He'd known all along she wasn't capable of leaving him!

Please, Matt. Meet me half way, don't make me grovel.

She took one step toward him, and stopped. Her eyes begged him to take a step toward her. He didn't. She took another step, and another. She kept taking little steps until she was inches from touching his body. Still he kept his arms crossed, but his eyes were filled with warmth and tenderness.

Her eyes filled with tears, imploring him to take her in his arms. Being careful not to let her body touch his, she placed a kiss on the corner of his mouth. He remained impassive. She softly kissed the other corner of his mouth, the underside of his neck.

She deeply inhaled his familiar scent before finally pressing herself into him, laying her head on his chest.

It was only then that he moved. He clutched her to him like he'd never let her go. His fingers worked their way through her curls, his other hand gently forced her head up so he could look at her beautiful face.

He bent his head and kissed her hungrily before whispering against her lips, "Please don't ever put me through that again. I don't want to think of my life without you in it."

Tears ran down Grace's cheeks and Matt kissed them away.

Grace thought about what a spectacle they were making, passionately hugging and kissing like they hadn't seen each other in years.

"Should we go?" Grace whispered.

"Just one more thing." He stepped away and reached into his pocket, took out her engagement ring and slipped it on her finger once again.

"Will you marry me Grace? Will you promise to stay with me till death do us part?"

"Oh, yes Matt. I do promise you. I've never been more sure of anything in my life."

Epilogue

The big day had finally arrived. Grace was doing her final primping in a little room in the back of the small church.

Janet quietly slipped in, eager to get her first peek at the bride. Grace looked radiant. Janet couldn't help but stare in wonder at the exquisite woman she and Brett had created.

Grace had Brett's clear green eyes, and though her hair was the same golden blond as her own, she had been blessed with Brett's dark eyelashes and eyebrows, too.

Other than her auburn hair, Faith had borne a striking resemblance to Janet, but Grace was a beautiful combination of them both.

What a shock it had been to learn she'd given birth to *two* baby girls on that day so long ago!

She ached for the daughter she'd never known, whose life had been taken all too soon, but she rejoiced in the fact that Faith had been brought up to love Jesus and had, from all accounts, lived a charmed life.

And at long last, her prayers were being answered for Grace, too. Grace exuded joy, positively glowed with the excitement of becoming Matt's wife and Ella's mother.

She grinned at Janet, doing a half twirl to show off her dress.

"So? What do you think?"

"I think you're breathtaking. Matt won't be able to keep his eyes off of you."

Grace made a quick perusal of Janet. She took in everything—her dress, her gorgeous hair, her carefully applied make-up. She looked youthful and beautiful.

"I have a feeling Jack will have a tough time keeping his eyes off of you, too. Actually, Brett might have a tough time as well."

Janet's face flushed, ashamed how much she wanted that to be true. But wasn't that normal? Wouldn't every woman want to look good for someone she had once loved but had been rejected for another woman?

Janet had forced herself not to ask Grace many questions about Brett. She never asked what he looked like or if Marilyn was just as beautiful as ever. Maybe he would be fat and bald, giving her another reason to be thankful she'd let him have his dream and his old girlfriend.

"Janet?" Grace broke into her thoughts. "Why *are* you so nervous about seeing him? It's been so long and you're both happily married. Are you afraid he's going to be rude to you? I told you he's forgiven you . . ."

There was sudden fire in Janet's blue eyes, "Forgiven me? He should *thank* me. I let him keep his dream, and his girlfriend."

"Well, for whatever reason, *he* doesn't see it that way, but it doesn't matter. The past is the past and we're all here together for this one wonderful day and I want you to relax and enjoy every minute of it."

Janet knew Grace was right, she walked over and cupped her hands gently on each side of her daughter's face, "I promise I will. It *is* a miracle how my prayer brought us all together."

"I know," Grace whispered. "I will never get over it."

Janet stared into her daughter's eyes that were so heartbreakingly like her father's, and then impulsively hugged her tightly. *Thank you, Jesus, for bringing my baby girl back to me and letting me be a part of this joyous day.*

Brett had promised Grace he would be on is best behavior upon seeing Janet for the first time after all these years. He agreed Grace and

Matt's wedding day was not the time nor the place to seek answers to his questions.

He waited impatiently outside the small room for Grace to emerge. He wanted to see her before she walked down the aisle. When she finally swept out, she took his breath away. He opened his arms to embrace her, then froze at the sight of Janet behind her. Their eyes met and Brett felt the same shock of attraction he'd felt all those years ago. It was as if time hadn't touched her. If anything she was even more beautiful. It took every ounce of will power to drag his eyes off of her and concentrate on Grace.

He recovered from his interrupted embrace by clutching Grace's shoulders and keeping her at arm's length, taking in the full length of her.

"Absolutely stunning! I've never seen a prettier bride . . ." He swallowed an unexpected lump in his throat.

Janet couldn't stop staring at Brett. She knew he must be feeling her gaze, yet after those first intense seconds when their eyes met, he acted like she wasn't there.

She struggled to suppress the long buried feelings she'd felt for him. Her face felt hot and her heart raced. He looked magnificent. His thick hair held touches of gray, but beyond that he looked the same. He was still the fit, muscular man he'd been at eighteen, just a little thicker through the shoulder's and chest. And those eyes! She remembered how those clear, green eyes use to look at her with such adoration. All the emotions he'd brought out in her as a teenager resurfaced at the sight of him.

Had she imagined the old longing she thought she'd glimpsed before he deliberately ignored her? Was he planning on ignoring her all night?

Still not acknowledging Janet, he tucked Grace's hand into the crux of his elbow.

"I think you have an anxious father waiting to escort you down the aisle, shall we go?"

Grace stopped Brett for a minute and gave him a gentle kiss on the cheek, "Thank you for being here," she whispered.

"I wouldn't miss it for the world."

The ceremony was beautiful. All the attendees knew the story behind their unlikely romance. No one could help but acknowledge God's hand in it.

As much as Janet wanted to concentrate solely on the beauty unfolding in front of her, she couldn't get beyond her acute awareness of Brett sitting in the same pew. Who would have thought they would ever share a pew?

She wondered about Brett's faith. She wondered if anyone had penetrated the wall he'd built around his heart. Was his wife a Christian? When Janet had taken her first surreptitious glance at her, she'd been shocked it wasn't Marilyn. What had happened to Marilyn? She never pictured Brett with anyone but her. And this woman was the antithesis of her. She was tall and athletically built, not petite and voluptuous.

Janet peeked down the pew at them now, noting the proprietary way Brett's wife clutched his hand, her opposite hand on his forearm. She wondered if Brett had ever talked about her *before* Grace showed up. Had he passed her off as a long forgotten teenage romance?

Brett tried focusing on the ceremony, too. He wanted only to marvel at the unlikely event of attending his *daughter's* wedding. But seeing Janet, looking just as beautiful as he remembered, had rattled him and he knew Patty could feel his tension.

Brett tried to put himself in Patty's shoes. Here they'd struggled all these years with infertility issues and then, out of nowhere, Grace shows up and claims he's her father. How had it made Patty feel to learn her beloved husband fathered a child many years ago with a woman he'd never mentioned, a woman who was still breathtakingly beautiful? It couldn't be easy. He gave her hand a reassuring squeeze.

After the ceremony, brief introductions were made. Jack enthusiastically grasped Brett's hand and congratulated him on the marriage of his beautiful daughter.

Of course, there was no need for introductions between Janet and Brett, and Brett continued to act like she wasn't even there.

Brett's icy demeanor left Janet with a sick feeling in the pit of her stomach. Was it guilt? All these years she'd thought she'd done Brett a favor by running away, but his attitude towards her indicated otherwise, and it made her heart heavy.

At the reception, Janet struggled to act normal. Jack did all he could to cajole her out of her uncharacteristic melancholy, but her heart felt constricted, her throat too tight to talk.

When dinner was over, a place was cleared for the dance floor. The dancing was Janet's favorite part of every wedding. She loved watching the first dance of the bride and groom, loved watching the bride dance with her father. She'd forgotten to ask Grace how she was going to handle the whole dance thing with Brett. Would she include him? Or just dance with the only father she'd ever known?

As the bride and groom's dance ended, Grace walked over and took her adoptive father's hand. The first chord to "Daddy's Girl" started and tears filled Janet's eyes. Listening to the words of the song and watching Grace and her father sway to the music drove home what Brett had missed out on. When Grace had told Janet Brett and his wife had never been able to have children, her heart had ached for them. Unwittingly, Janet had robbed Brett of his only opportunity to be a daddy.

When the song ended, Grace kissed her father before turning to Brett. He offered his hand gallantly before whirling her expertly around the dance floor. They danced to an upbeat, fast dance tune and the guests loved it, enthusiastically cheering them on.

When the music slowed, Ella ran out to join them, tugging on Brett's arm, "Dance with me! Dance with me!" Brett swept her up and held her close against him before putting her back down and taking her little hands in his and dancing around the floor with her.

Janet had been surprised how close Brett and Grace had become in the short span of time they'd been reunited. But then again, they lived close to each other, so it shouldn't be so surprising. They spent a lot of time together.

Even before Brett and Patty discovered Brett was actually Ella's biological grandfather, they'd treated her like their own grandchild, spoiling her rotten with everything their little princess desired.

After all the members of the bridal party danced, the rest of the guests were asked to join them. On the dance floor, Jack pulled Janet close and whispered how beautiful she looked, how proud he was of her. As soon as the song ended, she wanted to head back to their seats. So unlike her, it was usually Janet coaxing Jack to stay out on the dance floor.

They'd only been seated a few moments before her breath caught in her throat. Brett was striding purposefully over to their table. Was he finally going to break his silence?

Still without looking at her, he asked Jack if he would mind if he danced with his wife.

Jack hesitated slightly, so unlike him, but nodded an assent. No words, no smile, just a nod.

Brett offered his hand and as soon as Janet took it she felt the old familiar thrill.

Janet recognized the old Elvis song they were playing, "Love Me Tender." Of all the songs! She wondered wildly if Brett knew what this particular song meant to her. To this day, whenever she heard it she couldn't help but remember that fateful day at the lake.

Brett deliberately guided them into the center of the throng of dancers. He pressed his hand into the small of her back and enclosed her hand gently in his, being careful to keep their bodies from touching. Janet placed her free hand lightly against his chest.

He finally met her eyes, with all the intensity she remembered. She couldn't break that gaze if she wanted to, and right now she didn't.

"Does this song mean anything to you?" he asked quietly.

Janet hesitated. *Of course it did!* But she would never admit that to him. It wouldn't be right. Instead, she forced herself to answer a little breathlessly, "It sure brings back memories from high school."

"Any *particular* memory?" he prodded, smiling sardonically.

She wanted to change the subject. Get on to something safer. It was too much, this song, being in his arms. Seeing him, smelling him. Remembering what it was like to be kissed by him. It was wrong and somehow it hurt, too. It hurt to know he could still have this effect on her, it was wrong that this song still had the power to send her back to that day that had changed her life forever. It was wrong his eyes could still hold hers, just as they used to.

His fingers grasped hers a little more firmly, "Why?"

When she didn't answer, he went on, "I promised Grace I wouldn't ask you any questions tonight, but this song started playing and it brought back memories and suddenly I wanted to know, I *needed* to know. *Why?*"

She knew what he was asking, but she wasn't ready to answer. Instead, she asked a question of her own, "What happened to Marilyn?"

"Marilyn who?" He looked so genuinely puzzled it made Janet smile. Seeing her dimpled smile again, made him smile.

"Silly. You know what Marilyn. Voluptuous little Marilyn you and every other guy couldn't stop ogling. All these years I'd just assumed you'd married her."

"Oh . . . *that* Marilyn. I'd forgotten about her. After I started dating you, every other girl paled in comparison. You were the only girl I loved in high school. You know that. Why would you think I would marry *her?* I only ever wanted to marry *you.*"

"You said I was the only girl you loved, but you didn't act like it."

"Didn't act like it? How could you say that? I could barely think about anything *but* you. I almost blew my scholarship trying to find you, trying to figure out what happened to us. I went half crazy. So, *please.* Tell me. *Why*?" he asked earnestly, his eyes pleading with her to make him understand.

"Because I went up to surprise you for lunch one day and when you weren't at the counter I walked around to find you, and I..." Janet closed her eyes remembering the pain, amazed how clearly she could still picture them—even after all these years. "I found you with Marilyn in your arms. That's why!"

"I don't believe it."

"Well! I didn't dream it up." Janet's tone got sharper. "It was devastating. I felt used and stupid for ever believing you truly cared about me. I thought after we did . . . *that,* that maybe you, that maybe, I don't know . . ." her voice trailed off, she didn't know how to explain what she'd felt and was uncomfortable alluding to their intimacy.

"I don't know what you could have seen. But I can promise you, *especially* after 'that,' as you call it, I knew you were the only girl for me."

Brett wracked his brain trying to think of what Janet might have seen, why he would've had Marilyn in his arms. Suddenly, it came to him.

"I bet she'd just told me her mom had cancer. Actually, I think her mom died right before Christmas that year."

Right around the time Janet gave birth to his babies!

They stopped dancing. Stopped and stared at each other, both thinking how those few ill- timed moments had changed the course of their lives forever. *If* she'd arrived a few minutes later, *if* Janet hadn't chosen that particular day, *if* Marilyn's mother hadn't gotten sick . . . oh, how different their lives would have been!

Brett still had his hand pressed into the small of her back, her hand still clutched tightly in his. He slowly took in every detail of her face, before meeting her eyes again.

She forced herself to take a step back. She tried to disengage her hand, but Brett held on.

"What about all the letters I wrote you? Your mother told me she'd make sure you got them."

"I never got any letters from you," Janet whispered hoarsely. *Why would Mama have withheld his letters from me?*

"Then your mother lied to me. She's just as much to blame that my daughters grew up not knowing me, who robbed me from knowing them . . . or loving you."

Janet's heart began to bubble with simmering resentment towards her mother, she had had no right to keep his letters from her! But if not for her mother's "interference," she wouldn't have Jack in her life *or* a houseful of beautiful children and all the precious memories of their life together.

"Even after I fell in love with Patty, I worried I might still have feelings for you, so I tried to find you one last time, and when your parents told me you were married and expecting a second child I knew it was time to let you and my memory of you go."

"I'm sorry, Brett. I did what I did because I loved you and didn't want to ruin your life. I didn't want you to have to give up your dream, I . . ."

"What you did was *wrong*. I deserved to have a say in it, but . . ."

Janet interrupted him before he could finish, "Well it can't be undone. Brett. Please understand. I was just a girl, I was madly in love with you and I was convinced you'd fallen out of love with me. I didn't think I'd ever get over it. But then I met Jack. He's wonderful, Brett. I used to worry I might not ever feel for him what I felt for you. And, at first, I didn't. But I do now. I wouldn't undo any of it, even if I could." She turned to walk away, but Brett clasped her shoulders and gently turned her to face him. He waited for her gaze to meet his one last time.

"You didn't let me finish. I wanted to let you know that I *have* forgiven you. I can even say I'm thankful you left me because if it weren't for my broken heart, I might never have accepted Jesus as Lord. My first college roommate not only *talked* about his faith, he *lived* it. He is the reason I first believed. He is the one who introduced me to Patty because he knew she was just what I needed. And she is. She is everything to me. Patty fell in love with Grace the first night she met her. You might think she'd feel resentful that a girl I once loved gave us the child we could never have, but that's not my Patty. Patty and I are *both* overwhelmed with gratitude for the miracle of being reunited with Grace and Ella. We know that if you hadn't written that prayer when you were just a broken-hearted young teenager it would never have happened. We thought we'd never experience parenthood and now, we not only have a daughter, but a grandchild as well."

Janet felt tears welling up at his words and Brett gave her shoulders a final squeeze and whispered, "Thank you," before turning and walking back to his beloved wife.

Janet slowly walked back to their table, to Jack. She willed her racing heart to slow down, for her hands to stop shaking.

She found Jack sitting by himself at the table. She knew he was aware of her slipping into the chair beside him, but he didn't look at her. He stared at a point in the distance, a muscle ticked in his jaw. She could feel his irritation.

"Jack?"

She knew he heard her, but still he didn't look at her. *Please Jack. Don't be hurt. Don't let this come between us.*

Janet studied his dear, familiar profile. How often had she traced that profile with her finger?

She loved the bump on the bridge of his nose, loved the strong set of his jaw.

She looked at his hands clasped on the table. She pictured those beautiful hands cradling the heads of each of their babies. He'd delivered all of them.

She pictured those hands putting toys together in the wee hours before Christmas morning. Most of all she pictured his hands on her body, instinctively knowing when and where to touch her, intimate with every nuance of her both physically and emotionally.

She hesitantly put her hand on his knee, imploring him to look at her.

Jack struggled not to be bothered. He didn't want to act jealous, didn't want to *be* jealous.

What did he have to be jealous about? Was he going to allow a teenage romance that ended more than a quarter of a century ago affect this beautiful night? What was he afraid of? He and Janet had been married for over a quarter of a century. They were wonderful years, too, filled with joy and sweet memories. Heck, if it hadn't been for this man and their ill-fated teenage romance, he would never have met Janet. He should feel nothing but gratitude. He *would* be grateful. He would rise above this. Janet was *his*, nothing would change that. He inhaled deeply, raked his hands through his hair and stood up. He looked down at his beautiful, beloved wife and offered her his hand.

"'Can I have this dance?'" he softly sang the words. His deep, beautiful voice pitch perfect.

Janet didn't answer immediately. She stood up and wrapped her arms tightly around him, pressing her body into his. She nuzzled his neck, breathing him in, before whispering in his ear, "Yes, Jack. You can have this dance . . . 'for the rest of your life.'"

The End

To those who made this book a reality—my husband Bob, the love of my life and my biggest cheerleader. My father, who left us for his eternal home way too soon. He always believed in me, praised everything I wrote and insisted I had a gift. My sweet daughter Caitlin and my brother Jeff, who not only spurred me on, but proofread my original manuscript, offering valuable suggestions and corrections. My precious friend Tammy, a gift who inspires me like no other. My sister-in-law Shannon, who never fails to encourage me. My friend Stacey, who shares my love for writing. My sister Kristie, who strongly encouraged me to start blogging. It was the encouraging words from my blog readers that ultimately allowed me to believe in myself as a writer. Though by no means an exhaustive list, those that come to mind are Dawn March, Linda Cummins, Peggy Golasa, Ellie Fogelberg, Kelly Dewaele, Carol Chilcoff, Linda Coffin Allen, Kelly Thweatt, Jennifer Krause, Lisa Sendo Staples-Farrough, Loretta Brothers, Gladys Lock, Dawn Amann Baker, Ted March, Sheila Nielson, Sarah Bechler, Debbie Davidson, Nora Weismiller, Kathleen Frost, Judy Walkin, Jackie Sanders, Jean Taylor, Patty Closser, Shannon Kelly Klopfenstein, Ann Smith, Cathy Jennings, Lynnette Underwood, Suzanne Dunphy, Sharon Isenegger, and Carolyn Amann—I thank you *all* from the bottom of my heart!

About the Author

Laurie Staples is an author, flight attendant, and mother of three. An avid reader and writer, she has long been blogging about her job experiences as a flight attendant for a major airline as well as her role as the mother of a severely impaired child. Those who read her blog, lauriestaples.blogspot.com, will find poignant stories that will make them both laugh and cry.

Staples received her bachelor's degree in English from Stetson University. With her two older children now grown, she lives with her husband, Bob, and Brett, her special-needs son, in Plymouth, Michigan.

Made in the USA
Columbia, SC
25 July 2017